I0761927

"I don't believe we've met," she said.

"I have to agree." I strained to see her through the darkness, but her chair was not only hidden in the shadows, it was turned away from my view.

"Why are you here?" I asked.

She hesitated.

"I'm hiding."

I laughed out loud before I caught myself.

"And who are you hiding from?"

"Handsy, self-absorbed, mind-numbingly dull suitors."

Suitors. I hadn't heard that word lately. Or handsy for that matter.

"I would hide from them, too," I said.

"What are you doing here?" she asked.

What was I doing here? Nothing really, when it came right down to it. My grandfather had called me here just so he could tell me that my sister had gone back in time.

I suppose he thought it would bring me closure.

"I'm looking for my sister," I said.

"Oh," Isabella said. "Is she lost?"

SCRIPTED IN THE STARS

ALSO BY KATHRYN KALEIGH

THE BECQUERELS

Twist of Fate

When the Stars Align

Once in a Blue Moon

Once Upon a Christmas

A Wish Upon a Star

Written in the Wind

Scripted in the Stars

Destined in the Twilight

Promised in the Mist

Trapped in the Melody

When Lightning Strikes

Storm of Time

Midnight Storm

When the Moon Falls

Stormborn Angel

Time Tempest

The Heart Remembers

A Moment in Time

Moonlight Shadows

Rescued in Time

SCRIPTED IN THE STARS

THE BEQUERELS

INTO THE MIST

KATHRYN KALEIGH

SCRIPTED IN THE STARS

PREVIEW: DESTINED IN THE TWILIGHT

Written by Kathryn Kaleigh

Published by KST Publishing, Inc., 2022

Cover by Skyhouse24Media

www.kathrynkaleigh.com

To learn more about Kathryn Kaleigh, visit

www.kathrynkaleigh.com

Kathryn Kaleigh

PROLOGUE

Jonathan Becquerel slipped his pry bar beneath the window frame in the guest room on the second floor of his house. Sophia's room.

He moved slowly. Methodically. Careful not to break the several hundred-year-old glass panes.

One of his favorite 80s songs blared through the air pods his granddaughter Sophia had ordered for him. She'd also created a play list of his favorite songs on his phone.

Considering that Jonathan lived in the country and mostly stayed to himself, he attributed his level of being modern and hip to his granddaughter's efforts.

Though it had only been hours since he saw her, he already missed her terribly.

He'd raised the window before going to work to let some fresh air in. The soft breeze brought the scent of daffodils with it. They were his favorite flower. Not necessarily because of how they looked, though he did prefer the white ones, but because of their strong scent.

Sometimes he'd cut some out of his garden and bring them inside. Their fresh scent would perfume the house for days.

Having the window open, however, was a much better option. It allowed the scent to fill the room without having to cut the flowers. He much preferred letting them live to cutting them.

With the window frame loosened, he nudged it out with the prybar. He winced when the wood cracked. Nothing less than was expected since the window frames in this room, like the glass, were hundreds of years old.

It didn't worry him, though. He could fix it easy enough.

Since it was already cracked, he just ripped it off, letting the wood crumble.

Along with the wood, a little roll of paper—alkaline paper—dropped out. She'd thought of everything. He remembered the day the alkaline paper had been delivered. It was the same day he'd received his first packet of white daffodil bulbs.

He and Sophia had spent the afternoon outside planting them. She had been quieter that day. It had only been later that he'd learned the true reason why she'd bought the alkaline paper. They said alkaline paper could last centuries without decomposing. How they'd known that was beyond Jonathan's comprehension.

Careful with the little slip of paper, much more careful than he had been with the window frame, he unrolled it and leaned back on the stool he sat on.

Then he began to read the familiar handwriting.

Dear Jonathan,

If you are reading this letter, then you know that I have gone back in time. It worked.

I so hope you found this letter. It makes me happy that you know I've made it to the past safely.

I didn't get to say goodbye and I'm sorry for that. But we talked about this and I know you understand. Still I miss you terribly and wish that you were here with me.

Please tell the rest of the family that I love them.

Take care of yourself and know that I love you.

Sophia

JONATHAN DROPPED HIS HANDS IN HIS LAP.

It was done then. Just as he'd known it would be.

Sophia resembled her grandmother—Jonathan's wife—in that way. And she had no man holding her here. She'd found her man in the past. Somewhere in the 1800s. His name was Nathan Laurent.

As much as he didn't want to, Jonathan knew what he had to do.

He pulled his cell phone out of his shirt pocket and scrolled through until he found his grandson's number.

It was a heavy heart that he called Cameron Becquerel.

Making this phone call drove home Jonathan's acceptance that this was real.

Sophia had really gone back in time.

1

CAMERON BECQUEREL

I drove my Maserati with the top down along the River Road.

I'd been on location in Memphis filming one of my screenplays when Grandpa Jonathan—my father's father—had called me.

Although he hadn't said what he needed to talk to me about, I already knew.

It had been a long time coming.

I turned down the one-lane dirt road leading to the Becquerel Estate and drove beneath the ancient oak trees with limbs so thick and heavy, they dipped all the way to the ground.

Silver gray moss clung to the trees, especially the older oaks for which they had an affinity.

A text message appeared on the dashboard in front of me.

MEGAN: *Call me sweetie. I miss you.*

Although she'd been unhappy about it, I'd left my girlfriend Megan back in Memphis.

She was upset that I wasn't bringing her to meet my Grandpa.

I'd tried to explain that he was old and in bad shape and didn't tolerate visitors.

It wasn't true of course.

Grandpa was eighty if he was a day and he was in better shape than some men half his age. His mind was good, too. He was very fortunate.

Truth was, I had some personal family business to discuss with Grandpa and I didn't want Megan to know about it.

That was the thing about working in Hollywood. I had to keep my real personal life to myself. I had, in effect, to be someone I wasn't.

Even Megan couldn't know who I really was.

The less my colleagues knew about my real personal life, the less ammunition they had to use against me.

I had a deep visceral reaction to seeing the house up ahead. It was a lovely southern Greek plantation house… hundreds of years old.

I'd thought several times about using it as a movie set. But again, as long as my Grandpa lived, which I hoped was forever, I would keep it away from my life as a screenwriter.

And Megan, one of the stars of the current film I was working on was part of the me I wanted to project to the world. A tall leggy blonde with a sultry, knowing smile. The star of my current project. Not that I was complaining. She was good in bed.

I pulled around behind the house and parked next to the back veranda. Grandpa had his garden back in shape again. Granted it was ten times smaller than it had been the last time I was here, but he'd obviously been working on it. That was a good sign.

I parked the car and hit the button to put the top up.

I halfway expected Grandpa to be sitting out on the veranda, but there was nothing but three empty white wooden rockers.

I knocked on the door and turned around, looking toward the river.

Only a glimpse of the river was barely visible from here, through the trees. The water glimmered beneath the setting sun, the first sign of the sunset to come.

I turned around as the door opened.

Grandpa stood there, a blank expression on his face and pushed the door open.

I stepped through and closed the door behind me.

We walked silently into the kitchen and stood looking at each other.

"Did they find her body?" I asked.

2

ISABELLA LAURENT

Near Natchez, Mississippi
May 1853

It was a beautiful clear night. The sun had dipped below the horizon leaving the moon to watch over us.

The Becquerel home was lit up like day light with candles and lanterns everywhere.

Fresh flowers filled the house with color and a sweet scent that tempered the scent of cigar smoke and the ham that had been smoking for most of the day, making my mouth water.

The grandfather clock began to chime the hour. I would have to go down soon. Actually I was already teetering on arriving too late.

Two of my brothers were already downstairs, no doubt finding some kind of trouble to get into.

My other brother, Nathan, was probably at his own home with his wife Sophia. Sometimes they came to the parties, sometimes they didn't. My brother Nathan was like me when it came to parties. He could live just fine without them.

I stood at the top of the stairs, out of the way, watching the guests as they arrived.

This was the third party my cousins had held in the last month, always eager to introduce me to eligible men.

Mon Dieu.

Didn't they understand that I was not in the market for a husband?

I had given some serious thought to hiding out in my cousin's garçonnière for the evening or maybe pleading off with a bad headache, but getting a new dress was worth enduring an evening of music.

Besides, Momma knew me well enough to keep me in check. I could get nothing past her.

This one had the widest hoop skirt I'd ever worn. And it had a million yards of silk cascading over it. But the best part was the perfect décolletage that revealed a scandalously large swatch of my creamy white skin. Wearing this dress, I felt all grown up and maybe, just maybe, I'd try out some of those feminine wiles my governess had been insisting that I learn.

Like she said, I didn't have to marry them or even let them court me just because I flirted a bit with them.

I sighed. If nothing else, it would help pass the time.

These soirees could be so tiresomely long. If I hadn't been certain that Momma would swat me on the head, I would have brought a book downstairs with me.

Momma allowed me a lot of leniencies, but that wasn't one she would tolerate. A lady always showed good manners, no matter what situation she found herself in.

"Miss?" Villars, the butler asked, coming up behind me. "Is there anything I can get for you?"

"No thank you Villars," I said.

Villars put his hands behind his back and stood still for a moment.

"It's a lovely night for a storm," he said.

Perplexed by his words, I turned to look at him, but he was walking away.

Whatever did he mean by that?

I shrugged and started downstairs.

I'd always found my cousins in the northern part of Mississippi to be somewhat strange and in the few months I'd lived here with my family, that had not changed.

However, being from New Orleans, I had a high tolerance for strangeness.

3

CAMERON

Grandpa heated water the old-fashioned way with a tea kettle on the stovetop.

Hot tea wasn't something I typically bothered with. I usually ended my day with a glass of red wine. But if there was one thing I'd learned working in Hollywood, it was to be flexible and low maintenance.

There was very little I despised more than a prima donna, especially in a man.

Being raised by a general had taught me at a very young age that a man's job was to be part of the team and to defer to authority or in this case authority would be synonymous with my elders.

The tea kettle whistled and Grandpa went over to turn off the flame. He moved a bit slower than I would have like to see.

Maybe he'd called me here about something other than my sister. Maybe he wanted to discuss his own health.

Grandpa was at that age when he needed to consider his options. I hated the thought of him having to leave here to go into assisted living. If he needed someone to come here to help him out, I could hire a live-in caregiver. We could either move his bedroom downstairs or put in an elevator.

I glanced around. My sister had been the architect. She was the one who would have known how to incorporate an elevator into a house like this.

Fortunately there were other architects and I could easily make it happen. If that was what he wanted.

"Do you get lonely out here?" I asked.

"What?" He turned around with two mugs of steaming hot tea. "Hardly. I have—"

He stopped in mid-sentence and slid into the chair across from me.

I had a sense, a tingling along my spine, that there was something else. Something he had to tell me.

Maybe it was because I wrote fictional scripts for a living. I had a tendency to look ahead for possibilities.

"There's something I need to tell you," he said. "Something that is probably long overdue." He slid one of the mugs over toward me.

I held the mug close and breathed in the minty scented steam with a new appreciation for hot tea.

"Does this have something to do with Sophia?"

My sister Sophia had gone missing ten years ago. It had shattered my family to the core.

But with time we'd gone forward. Moved on with our lives.

In some ways it had made us closer, but in other ways it had put a wall between us.

Even though it had happened here, under Grandpa's watch so to speak, he'd been overall quiet. He'd called me.

Our mother lived in France with her new husband and my father, still wrapped up in military retirement, was starting a new life as well, with his new wife.

As the oldest of four siblings, responsibility tended to fall on my shoulders anyway, so I was used to it.

But dealing with the disappearance of my sister was another thing entirely.

I'd never been the same.

"Yes," he said, obviously stalling.

"Grandpa," I said. "Just tell me. Whatever it is, I can handle it. I've come to terms with the reality that she will not be coming back.

Grandpa sipped his tea and looked into my eyes. He didn't believe me. Whatever it was, it was so bad he didn't believe I could handle it.

I braced myself. Prepared for the worst. The worst I could think of was they'd found her body in the woods or the river. Though how that had happened after ten years was more than I could imagine.

"She went back in time," he said.

4

ISABELLA

Music from the little three-man orchestra kept the dancers on the floor. The weather was perfectly mild and the French doors along one side of the room were wide open to allow fresh air to flow in and people to spill out onto the veranda.

My dance card filled up within minutes. Unfortunately, I received a lot of scathing glances from other ladies as a result. I truly wished they knew I would much rather be in their shoes. In fact, it seemed like the more I tried to push the suitors away, the more they flocked in my direction.

My first waltz of the night was with a tall, lanky fairly handsome man who talked nonstop about his experiences with gambling on the riverboats. After about two of his stories, I was ready to talk about something else. I had no interest in gambling.

And if I had been looking for a husband, I certainly wasn't looking for one who would doubtless leave his wife at home in order to seek out the thrill of an escapade on the riverboats.

Besides, I'd only danced with him in order to test out my skills at flirtation.

This man barely noticed me at all, he was so enchanted with himself.

When he offered me punch and stroll on the veranda, I quickly declined and disengaged from him.

The second man was hardly any better. In many ways, he was the opposite of the first man.

This second man was hardly anything to look at. In fact, I found myself searching for something—anything—about him that I found attractive.

Momma assured me that he came from a good family, but there was most certainly more to a man than the family he was born into.

He had no stories to tell me. He was a man of very few words and two left feet. As I hadn't seen him around before, I was pretty sure he rarely attended social events.

I quickly disengaged myself from him as well.

The third man I danced with could only be described as handsy. His hands along my back going much too low on my waist. I kept my gaze away from him so as not to encourage him and I certainly did not dare to flirt with him. In fact, my older brother, Grant, cut in about halfway through to dance to rescue me from the man.

Feeling deflated and justified in returning to my usual standoffishness, I took some punch and went out on the veranda to get some air.

Just as I finished my glass of punch, I saw the gambler headed my way.

I ducked around through one of the other open doors and headed down the hallway.

It was quieter on this side of the house and much cooler since there were no people and fewer lights.

I blew out a breath of relief. My little foray into the world of courtship had gone just terribly.

It would be some time before I would fall for that again. If ever.

I ducked into the library shrouded in darkness and found an armchair to drop into.

I would simply sit here until the guest had left. Or maybe I could slip out the back door and use the stairs out back that led up to the balcony. I could get to my room that way.

Momma had seen me dancing, so should be satisfied enough to leave me be. At least for a little while.

I knew exactly what she would say. *A good start.*

I scoffed. A good start to staying away from the dance floor.

When… and if… I decided to get married, I would find someone who was not handsy, did not talk about himself all the time, and could carry on a conversation.

With three brothers, I knew quite well that a man was capable of these three simple things.

Having decided, I leaned back and closed my eyes.

5

CAMERON

Grandpa and I had talked late into the night. He'd sat at the little breakfast table with four wooden chairs while I paced around the kitchen. My brain just about ready to explode.

We'd talked through a light dinner. Sandwiches we threw together.

Apparently my sister, Sophia, had spent several months here with Grandpa, and a few days at most back in the 1800s.

She had quite simply lost ten years.

But not really lost. She'd just sort of skipped them. Darted into what for her was the future, then returned to the past for what Grandpa believed was for good.

During the few months she was back here, Grandpa had kept her hidden. I suppose that made sense as far as one could make sense out of time travel.

The only inconsistency I could find in Grandpa's story was that although he knew—was pretty sure—she'd gone back in time, he had still reported her missing.

He really had no choice. There was her apartment. Her job. Me. Our sisters.

If he hadn't reported her missing, someone would have come looking for her anyway.

The police had scoured the area, looking for her, and Grandpa had had no choice other than to let them.

It was truly an impossible situation and I did not want to be in his shoes. Not one bit.

But how was it possible that all this had been going on around me and I had no idea?

Time travel.

Grandpa had grown tired and had gone up to bed around eight o'clock.

I'd gone to his study and settled in to read Grandpa's notes and to reread the letter Sophia had left for him behind a window sill.

Those two were partners in crime. That's what they were.

There was a second note, too, that had been added to the first.

Dear Grandpa,

Nathan and I are married now and we have three children. Two boys and a girl. We have another on the way. Can you believe it?

I am so happy. When I'm not caring for the children, I sketch out house plans. I may never use them, but it keeps my mind occupied.

All my love,

Sophia

Even with my overactive imagination, I could not have written a more messed up convoluted story.

I must have fallen asleep, my head on his desk.

I woke slowly with music in the background. Orchestra music. A small orchestra. At first I thought I must have fallen asleep on the movie set. But this was not the set of any movie I had ever been on before.

And it didn't take long for me to realize I was in my grandfather's study and the electricity must have gone out.

Maybe Grandpa was playing some old music.

"Is someone there?"

Lifting my head from the desk, I scrambled for my phone, but couldn't find it where I thought I'd left it lying on the desk.

The music was one thing, but who was here in the house? Grandpa hadn't said anything about anyone else living here. We hadn't talked about anything other than Sophia and the time travel.

If this area was a time portal, then perhaps people just came and went between different times at will.

"Yes," I said, then cleared my rough voice that came out rough.

"I apologize," she said. "I can go."

Whoever this woman was, she had the voice of an angel. I knew as well as anyone that a person's voice didn't always match the way they looked, but this woman wasn't supposed to be here.

If she was from the past, then I most definitely wanted to talk with her.

"No," I said. "Please don't leave." I sat up straighter, but didn't leave my chair.

I didn't want to startle her away.

"What is your name?" I asked.

"Isabella."

A most beautiful name. A beautiful name that matched a beautiful voice.

"Isabella?" I asked.

"Isabella Laurent."

Laurent. I had cousins by that name.

My heart beat faster, pounding my blood through my veins.

"My name is Cameron," I said. "Cameron Becquerel."

I heard her quick intake of breath.

"I don't believe we've met," she said.

"I have to agree." I strained to see her through the darkness, but her chair was not only hidden in the shadows, it was turned away from my view.

"Why are you here?" I asked.

She hesitated.

"I'm hiding."

I laughed out loud before I caught myself.

"And who are you hiding from?"

"Handsy, self-absorbed, mind-numbingly dull suitors."

Suitors. I hadn't heard that word lately. Or handsy for that matter.

"I would hide from them, too," I said.

"What are you doing here?" she asked.

What was I doing here? Nothing really, when it came right down to it. My grandfather had called me here just so he could tell me that my sister had gone back in time.

I suppose he thought it would bring me closure.

"I'm looking for my sister," I said.

"Oh," Isabella said. "Is she lost?"

6

ISABELLA

I had ducked into the library in order to be alone. I could still hear the orchestra music coming from the ballroom, but otherwise I was in a quiet room.

A room that smelled like cigars and leather books. It was truly my favorite room in the house.

But I was not alone.

There was a gentleman in here with me. Somewhere in the darkness behind me.

He said his name was Cameron Becquerel, so he had to be somehow related to my cousins. Yet I had never met him, nor had I heard of him.

Our two families were close. Close enough that I should have heard of him, no matter how distant a relative he was.

Our families spent summers together. Our family would pack up and travel north only to spend the long hot summers here at the Becquerel Estate.

I had never liked it. I much preferred to stay at our town home in New Orleans.

Cameron sounded pleasant enough. Yet neither one of us was supposed to be in here.

"Yes," he said. "My sister is missing."

"I'm so sorry to hear that," I said. "What are you going to do?"

"I really don't know," he said. "I don't think there's anything I can do."

"Surely there's something," I said, sitting up.

The thought of this man having a missing sister was quite unsettling.

"How old is she?" I asked.

"She's an adult," he said. "a little bit younger than me."

"Oh." Well. That might change things a little bit.

"Maybe she isn't missing," I said.

"What do you mean?"

"I mean..." I placed a hand over my eyes. How was I supposed to voice the most improper thing I was thinking?

"I mean maybe she meant to go. Maybe you just think she is missing."

Cameron didn't answer. I turned and tried to see him in the darkness, but the shadows were too much.

"That's actually very possible," he said.

I blew out a breath, relieved that he hadn't asked me to explain myself.

It would have been a most improper thing for me to discuss with a strange man.

Nonetheless, I wasn't ready to let the topic go. I was intrigued by it.

Perhaps I was intrigued by him, but that was something I'd have to think about later.

"How long has it been since you saw her?" I asked.

"A very long time ago," he said.

"A week? A month?"

The leather chair squeaked as he shifted in the chair.

"Ten years," he said, softly.

"Ten years," I repeated, slowly. "That's a very long time."

How was it that a woman could be missing for ten years?

"It is, isn't it?"

"Are you just now looking for her?" I asked. It was truly none of my business, but I truly wanted to understand.

"Oddly enough," Cameron said. "I think I might know where she is. Sort of."

I was truly confused by this man's answers.

It was fortunate that I was accustomed to strangeness.

7

CAMERON

The grandfather clock began to chime just as the music stopped.

Now I could hear people talking. It definitely caught me off balance for a minute, but then I realized maybe Grandpa was watching something on the television.

Or maybe he had his television set to come on automatically. That was possible. And would have been smart.

I should probably and would probably have gotten up to go check, but I didn't want to leave. Not just yet.

I found myself wanting to answer Isabella. To spill everything about Sophia, but I had to be careful.

I didn't know this woman and I didn't want Grandpa to be taken away to the mental hospital. Besides that, I had a reputation to protect.

Hollywood was a funny place and if word got back to anyone that I had a time traveling sister—or even, maybe especially thought I did, it would spread like wildfire. I'd probably never get another job in the industry.

So I had to find a way to talk to her without telling her directly about Sophia.

"If you know where she is," Isabella said. "Can you… talk to her?"

"I don't know for sure," I said.

Was I lying outright? Did I know for sure that I couldn't talk to Sophia? If she was truly in the past, then no, I couldn't talk to her.

But if what Grandpa said was true, then maybe I could. If she were to come back to the present.

According to Grandpa, people who carried the Becquerel blood carried a spell. A spell that was used to save my Grandmother Vaughn's life in the 1700s.

She had just arrived in America and was on her way to marry a man she had never met when her traveling party was set upon by Indians.

Vaughn was the only person who survived.

An old Indian had placed a spell on her that had created a rip in time that had saved her life. So she had survived by going through time.

But there had been a catch. The spell that had saved her life had never healed. Vaughn continued to travel back and forth through time for the rest of her life.

And those of her blood, as Grandpa had put it, were also susceptible to traveling through time. It seemed especially likely if they came here to this house. Or maybe this area. Grandpa was a bit unclear about that part.

I was about to tell Isabella something, though whatever it was completely left my brain as the electricity came back on lighting up the room.

Jarred out of a haziness that had settled over me, I immediately stood up and went around behind the desk to find Isabella.

She wasn't there.

I stepped into the quiet hallway and looked right and left.

There was absolutely no way she could have vanished that quickly.

I walked past the grandfather clock in the foyer. It wasn't ticking now. It was just standing there. Wasn't it still broken?

Not having an answer, I walked into the parlor and stood in front of the television.

If the electricity was out, how was the television on earlier?

8

ISABELLA

"What do you mean you don't know?" I asked.

The chiming of the grandfather clock lingered a moment, mixing with conversations coming from the ballroom.

Cameron didn't answer me.

Maybe he was thinking.

I looked back again, squinting through the darkness, but I still couldn't see him.

"How do you not know?" I asked again. "Did you try?"

Silence.

The orchestra began playing again. A waltz this time.

"Cameron?"

Silence.

"There you are." My brother Grant walked into the room, carrying a bright lantern that lit up the room as he walked inside.

I stood up, took the lantern from him and held it high with one hand as I walked through the room holding up my skirt with the other.

"Where is he?" I asked.

Grant stood behind me now.

"Where is who?"

"Cameron," I said. Maybe he'd gone outside.

I went over to the one French door in the room. The clasp was locked. There was no way he could locked it from the outside.

Making a full turn around, I looked accusingly at my brother.

"Did you see Cameron leave here?"

"Who the he—who is Cameron?" he asked, purposely toning down his language.

I rolled my eyes at him. As one of my three older brothers, he knew full well I'd heard far worse, especially from our youngest brother, Andrew.

Andrew said pretty much whatever he wanted. I'd led a sheltered life overall, but I knew how men talked to each other.

"A man," I said. "He was here."

Grant bristled. "You were alone in here with a man?"

"We talked" I said. "but I didn't see him." I ignored his misplaced protectiveness. I didn't have time for that right now. I was far more concerned with where Cameron was.

Cameron was the one gentleman here that I could actually have a conversation with. It didn't even matter that the conversation hadn't exactly made a whole lot of sense.

At least he'd talked to me without talking all about himself and his gambling escapades. He'd been anything but handsy since he'd literally been sitting across the room from me.

"What was his name again?" Grant asked.

"Cameron," I said, handing the lantern back to my brother. "Becquerel."

"Never heard of him," Grant said. "Mother's looking for you."

"I'm sure she is," I said, under my breath, but I dutifully followed my brother toward the door.

"She wants to introduce you to someone."

I stopped, my feet freezing to the floor.

"Another man?"

"A gentleman planter from… somewhere," he said. "I forget where exactly."

"Well, if you don't know anything about him, why would I want to meet him?"

Drake turned and looked at me.

"Because I know that you'll simply appease mother by meeting him and going on your way. I'm not worried about you getting to know him."

"Why would you say that?" I asked.

"Isabella," he said. "You've made your views clear. You have no interest in being courted by anyone, much less getting married."

I followed my brother from the room. He was right.

I had made my views known to anyone who would listen.

No interest in getting married.

Marrying someone up here would tie me to this place and prevent me from returning to New Orleans.

There was only one problem with these assertions I'd repeatedly made over the past year or so.

I'd just spoken to a man that I did actually want to meet.

A man I might want to get to know.

9

CAMERON

I got up early the next morning after a sleepless night and made my way downstairs to the kitchen to start a cup of coffee.

Following my conversation with the phantom girl, Isabella, I'd gone up to bed.

I'd spent too long talking to Grandpa about time travel. So much that it had started to mess with my head.

Since Grandpa had no creamer, I poured coffee into a mug and added two packets of sweetener I found in a drawer.

I'd been dreaming, I decided, as I stirred the coffee.

I'd imagined the chiming clock, the voices, the music.

And I'd imagined the conversation with the girl named Isabella.

There was no other logical explanation. It had been one of those lucid dreams.

Sometimes when I was in the middle of writing a screenplay, if I had writer's block, I'd dream a solution.

Though I had to admit that I had never dreamed anything as clear as that conversation I'd had in the dark with a young lady named Isabella.

Only I wasn't in the middle of writing anything new at the moment. I was in the middle of working with the crew filming something I'd written months ago.

My… dream… was simply a manifestation of all that talk of time travel.

I'd dreamed the clock. I'd dreamed the voices.

And damn it, I'd dreamed the girl.

I didn't even know what she looked like, but I had held a conversation with her. About Sophia mostly.

I smiled at Isabella's trouble with suitors and how she'd been hiding from handsy, self-absorbed, mind-numbingly dull men.

It could be the start of a good idea for a movie if done right.

Good movies had started with less from my subconscious.

I took my coffee mug and went back into the study.

I went around and sat down at the desk where I'd fallen asleep last night and looked around for a chair the girl could have been sitting in.

She'd been sitting over to the left. Somewhere between the desk and the door. There was nothing there but Grandpa's old trunk.

The only chair in the room was over to the right.

Maybe she'd been sitting on the trunk… but I think I would have seen her. Surely. Even in the shadows.

I shook my head, stood up, and went to stand at the window.

There was something I had been meaning to do anyway.

I'd been meaning to dig through Grandpa's old leather trunk.

He'd told me it was okay to look at anything I wanted, so I took him at his word.

Kneeling in front of the trunk, so old it would have made a perfect movie prop, I opened the lid and let it fall against the wall.

There were lots of letters and some needlepoint—samplers —someone had taken the time to painstakingly create. I took a moment to appreciate the handiwork. As good as any machine could do. Brightly colored flowers. Birds. Butterflies.

I carefully moved those aside, looking for something, though I wasn't quite sure what exactly.

But when I found a stack of black and white tin photographs, I knew I'd found what I was looking for.

Taking a pair of reading glasses out of my shirt pocket, I sat back on my heels, and began to go through, looking closely at each one.

I looked carefully for an image of my sister.

If she'd gone back in time, surely there would be some evidence. Some photo of her somewhere.

Apparently she'd had three or four children, something I had trouble imagining for my sister who had never even had so much as a serious steady boyfriend.

Some of the photographs had names written on the back. It was mostly faded, but I could make out some of the names. None of which I recognized.

After going through about ten of the photographs, I came to a portrait of a young lady. She had long brunette hair pulled up on top of her head, a few long strands escaped to frame her face.

She had classically beautiful features. High cheek bones. Long lashes. And she photographed like a movie star.

Holding my breath, I turned the photograph over for a name or a date.

It was blank.

With a sigh, I sat back on my heels.

I knew what I'd been hoping.

I'd been hoping she was Isabella.

10

ISABELLA

The next morning, I sat in the parlor watching the flames greedily licking at the logs in the fireplace. One of the logs fell off the others, sending sparks up the chimney.

My cousin, Emma, sat at the piano playing what sounded like a waltz. A much more lively tune than I would have chosen.

I picked up the embroidery hoop in my lap and stabbed the needle through the cloth. The hoop held the material taut, almost too taut. I'd had one rip once, so I was careful.

Needlepoint was a questionably productive activity to begin with. I didn't want to have what I'd done so far go to waste.

I held up the design. This one was of yellow daffodils. I'd add a couple of blue and green butterflies along the top for some added color.

I would much rather be reading a book. My mother, however, insisted that a lady be proficient at several skills, needlepoint and piano included, in order to attract a husband.

She struggled to understand how I was content to sit through an entire day, from sunup to sundown reading a book.

But those days were the best. Especially those cold days that started off with frost on the ground, like today, and stayed chilly, unlike today.

May was like that. It could start off with perfectly chilly weather, frost on the ground, but it could go either way. Hot and sultry or perfectly comfortable weather.

Though others would disagree, I found it to be hotter up here in the northern part of Mississippi than it was in New Orleans. The air was more still up here. Less breezy.

My thoughts wandered their way around and settled at the same place they had been since last night.

On Cameron. I didn't even know what he looked like, but was the most interesting man I'd ever talked with.

We'd been talking about his sister when he simply vanished. I had to confess that I had kept looking for him since that night. But neither of my brothers who were at the party had ever heard of him.

I hadn't had a chance to ask Nathan, my other brother about him because he was with his new wife. But the first time I saw him I would ask him.

Nathan had lived up here longer than any of the rest of my immediate family had. Long enough to build himself a house within walking distance and besides that, he'd married a Becquerel. Perhaps he had met him.

It was possible that Cameron was even some of his wife's people.

"Isabella?" Mother asked. "Are you going to answer me?"

"What?" I asked, startled out of my thoughts.

"I asked what you thought about Theodore."

Theodore. The man mother had introduced me to right after I'd talked with Cameron.

"I'm sure he's a perfectly good man," I said, just wanting

Momma to leave me alone. In trust, I'd hardly paid him any mind. I had still been thinking about Cameron. I'd been looking for him, too even I didn't know who I was looking for.

If I could just hear his voice, I would recognize him.

I was certain of it.

He sounded so kind and even though I knew it was impossible, he'd sounded handsome.

Momma was still talking.

"That's good," she said because I invited him over for dinner tomorrow."

I dropped my embroidery hoop back into my lap and closed my eyes.

Mon Dieu.

Did Momma never stop?

I had zero interest in Theodore.

"Oh," I said. "Maybe Theodore and Grant will get along well."

"I'm sure they will," Momma said, with a gleefulness that made me apprehensive. "But even more important, I think the two of you will get along just fine."

There was really nothing I could say. When Momma took something in her head, there was no stopping her.

At least there had been nothing immediately offensive about Theodore.

Except, of course, that he wasn't Cameron.

11

CAMERON

"How long will you be able to stay?" Grandpa asked after my phone chimed with a text message.

MEGAN: *Are you ok? Missed talking to you last night.*

"I'm not sure," I told Grandpa. I could take a few days off the set without any problem. When I'd taken off down here, I hadn't known how long I would be gone, so I hadn't given them any expectations.

ME: *I'm good. Cell service is spotty.*

It wasn't the truth. And I wasn't prone to lying, but in some cases, it seemed to be called for. Like this one. I'd actually turned off my phone last night so I wouldn't have to talk to Megan.

It wasn't that I minded talking to her. She was interesting enough. It was just I had a lot on my mind.

My sister, of course, and learning that when she'd disappeared ten years ago, she'd actually gone back in time.

That was enough in itself.

Then there was Isabella.

I was pretty sure I was too old to have a psychotic break. I'd have to ask my sister, Victoria, the psychologist. She would know.

But I wasn't ready to admit to anyone, maybe especially not her, that I'd invented a whole new person in my head.

And this one wasn't even a character in a screenplay. I wasn't one of those writers who claimed to speak to their characters.

Writers who claimed to have that happen gave all writers a bad name in my opinion. That wasn't how it worked.

But maybe I'd been wrong.

Maybe it did happen that way.

Now I found myself thinking about writing a time travel screenplay staring a woman named Isabella Laurent.

"Stay as long as you want," Grandpa said.

In spite of his claim that he didn't get lonely out here, I didn't see how he could avoid it.

"Thank you," I said. "It was nice having Sophia here, wasn't it?"

"I miss her already," Grandpa's eyes misted up.

It was hard to comprehend that Grandpa had seen my sister just days ago, yet it had been ten years since I'd seen her.

"Are you getting along out here by yourself?" I asked. I was aware that it was a delicate question to ask, but after Sophia's disappearance, Father and his new wife had changed their minds about moving out here.

The house they'd started construction on was no more than a pile of rubble.

It was going to need to be cleaned up one day.

It looked like all this responsibility was going to fall on my shoulders.

"I did better when Sophia was here," Grandpa admitted. "I'm thinking of maybe looking to hire someone to come out stay with me."

I sighed in relief. "Not a bad idea," I said. "Need some help looking for someone?"

"I wouldn't mind it," Grandpa said.

"I'll get the process started," I said.

Helping Grandpa find a live-in caregiver was going to take some time.

ME: *I'm going to be awhile. Helping Grandpa with some stuff.*

MEGAN: *Ok. Sweetie.* I could hear the pout coming through the text message.

ME: *You'll be ok until I get back.*

I turned off my phone again and slid it in my pocket. Grandpa had just given me something to do.

And it might take me a couple of weeks at least to get him set up with someone.

And I found myself smiling to myself.

Staying here gave me that much more time to interact with Isabella again.

Even if she was part of my imagination.

12

ISABELLA

I'd been feeling antsy all through dinner. The closer it got to nightfall, the more restless I got.

I paced across my room to the window and pressed my cheek against the cool glass.

The full moon was hidden behind the clouds for the most part, but there was enough light that I could see the outline of the garden below. The scent of magnolia blossoms drifted through the slightly open window.

Emma was downstairs, still playing the piano. When she stopped, finally, everyone would start heading up to bed.

I was sharing a room with Emma since our family was boarding with the Becquerels until we could build a house of our own.

As far as I know, that process hadn't even started.

Accustomed to having my own space, I took advantage of evenings like this to have some time alone.

But tonight I was antsy for another reason.

Tonight, as soon as everyone, especially Emma, was asleep, I was going to make my way downstairs to the library.

I'd been thinking about Cameron all day.

I didn't understand what had happened to him… where he had disappeared to.

So I was determined to return there. To see if he returned.

The music stopped.

Finally.

Emma was a ham and my parents were her new audience.

I still wore my light green day dress.

I ran across the room, climbed into my side of the bed, and pulled the covers up to my chin.

Emma came in, humming to herself as she got undressed and into her nightgown.

I lay very still, waiting for her steady breathing to start telling me she was asleep.

When I heard her first little snore, I tossed the blankets off me, and slid out of bed.

Not daring to put on shoes, I walked across the room wearing only a pair of wool socks.

I slowly opened the door and, staying close to the edge of the wall, made my way to the stairs.

As I walked down the stairs, the grandfather clock began to chime the hour. It was already ten o'clock.

Mon Dieu. They had stayed up late.

I heard men's voices coming from the back veranda. They were smoking their nightly cigar before bed. My Aunt Eloise didn't tolerate cigar smoking in the house. Said it made everything too hard to clean.

My father and uncle would go from the veranda up to bed while my brothers and cousins would go to their garçonnière for the night.

I'd been there, to their bachelor's quarters a couple of times, but they just drank a lot and talked a lot of rubbish.

Not really how I liked to spend my evenings.

After ducking into the library, I sat down in the same chair I'd sat in last night.

It was dark, just like last night. I looked over my shoulder, toward my uncle's desk, but couldn't see anything.

I adjusted my skirts, clasped my hands in my lap and waited.

13

CAMERON

I'd spent some time during the day making some preliminary calls to an agency that could help me find someone for my grandfather's care.

I'd also started work on a new screenplay. Just something I was toying with.

I stirred the spaghetti sauce on the stovetop, then pulled a tray of garlic bread out of the oven and slid one onto a plate to hand to Grandpa.

"Didn't know you were such a good cook," Grandpa said.

"I get by," I said. "Being a bachelor and all."

"I know what you mean," Grandpa said.

I'd never thought of my grandpa being a bachelor, but I suppose being a widower had some similarities.

I heaped noodles onto two plates. Added sauce and cheese.

Grandpa and I sat at the kitchen table eating in silence for a few minutes.

"Do you ever think you hear things in this old house?"

Grandpa set his fork down and looked warily at me.

"Like what?"

"I don't know," I said, twirling spaghetti on my fork. "Like maybe the clock chiming or… music."

Grandpa leaned back. Shook his head.

"No," he said. "I don't. But I'm not one of Vaughn's descendants."

"Things get complicated, don't they? On the family tree."

"Don't even try to figure it out," Grandpa said.

I had tried. I couldn't help myself.

When I didn't answer, Grandpa looked at me sideways.

"Don't do it," he said. "it'll give you a headache."

I laughed.

"You heard these things?" he asked. "last night?"

Jonathan would know these things. He would have answers.

"What does it mean?" I asked.

"You carry Vaughn's blood," he said. "maybe you visited the past."

It startled me to hear him say the words out loud. My thoughts had swirled near the idea, but hadn't formed coherently in that direction.

"Maybe," I said, standing up. "Can I get you something else?"

"No," Grandpa said. "I think I'll just head upstairs. Turn in early."

I cleaned up the kitchen as Grandpa went upstairs to get some rest.

It was definitely a good idea to get someone out here to help Grandpa. This place was too big for him to handle alone. And he needed companionship.

With nothing left to do in the kitchen, I went back into the study and took my seat behind the desk.

I went to work on my screenplay and quickly lost track of time.

When I looked up again, it was dark.

I went over to the liquor cabinet, filled a glass with bourbon, and took it back to the desk with me.

Before going back to work, I turned on my cell phone and checked my messages. I had a message from my sister Victoria.

She was the one who held the three of us together after Sophia's disappearance. I would have to tell her about our sister. About the time travel.

But not now.

Later.

Maybe I would call her and Mackenzie out here and we'd all talk about it. I would need Grandpa to answer questions.

I certainly could not.

I assured her I was well. That Grandpa well was.

Then I dealt with the messages from Megan. All two dozen of them.

That was the trouble with dating a movie star. She expected to be the center of my world all the time.

Usually I didn't have a problem with that. When I was working, she was working.

She was the perfect arm candy.

I assured her I was busy with Grandpa. Busy with writing. I'd let her know when I was coming back to the set when I knew. I told her all that in the sweetest way possible.

Then I turned off the phone and got back to work.

14

ISABELLA

I woke when the book I'd been reading fell out of my lap onto to the floor with a crash. The little candle I had lit on the table next to me to read by had gone out.

It was quiet in the house and felt late. I must have been sleeping for some time.

I bent over to pick up my book. It was time for me to go up to bed.

I'd been fanciful to think that Cameron would still be here. He had no doubt returned to his own home.

"Hello?"

I gasped, holding the book to me like a shield.

It was like a shield.

"Cameron?" I asked, not believing that he was actually here.

"Isabella." I liked the way he said my name. It rolled off his tongue like a caress.

"I didn't think you were coming," I said.

"I'm here."

A logical woman would get up, light a candle, and go to him.

But this was not one of those logical situations and I never claimed to be a logical woman.

"Did you find your sister?" I asked, then bit my lip. Perhaps I was being insensitive.

"Not yet," he said.

We sat in silence a moment and I wondered if he had disappeared again.

"Do you live here?" he asked.

"Sort of," I said.

"Sort of," he repeated, his voice rough.

"For now," I clarified.

The clock chimed the hour. It was one o'clock.

Mon Dieu.

I had stayed up half the night.

If Momma knew or any of my family for that matter knew I was up in the middle of the night, alone, nonetheless, with a strange man, they would have me married to him in an instant.

"Isabella?"

"Yes?" I held my breath, waiting to hear what he would ask of me.

"Did you just hear the clock chime one time?"

"Yes," I said, my breath catching in my throat. "Didn't you?"

"I did... but..."

"But?"

"The clock is broken."

"No," I said, confused. What was he talking about? "The clock is working as it always is."

He was silent. I turned and squinted in the darkness, trying to see him.

The clouds shifted, letting a little bit of moonlight shine through the window.

I gasped as I caught a glimpse of a man sitting at my uncle's writing desk.

It was just a glimpse and then he was in darkness again.

"Isabella?"

"Yes?"

"I need to ask you something."

I nodded, then remembered he couldn't see me.

"Okay," I said.

"What year is this?"

"1853," I said. "Why do you—?"

A rumble of thunder overhead startled me.

"I have to go," I said, standing up and rushing from the out of the room to the hallway.

I didn't stop until I got back to Emma's bedroom.

I climbed into bed, careful not to disturb Emma.

Laying very still, I stared at the ceiling, taking slow deep breaths, waiting for my heartrate to slow down.

15

CAMERON

I sat at the desk in darkness as thunder crashed overhead.

I squeezed my eyes tightly closed as I tried to make sense of what I had just learned.

Not only had Isabella—the woman born of my imagination—just told me that the year was 1853, but I swear I just saw a woman wearing a long dress, run from the room.

I slowly put a hand on the desk, hoping to find my computer, but it was not there.

It had happened again. Whatever *it* was.

Grandpa had suggested that perhaps I had gone back in time.

It made perfect sense as far as explanations went. My sister had gone back in past. Why not me?

I'd heard the grandfather clock.

My computer… my phone… were no longer on the desk.

I'd talked to the girl—Isabella—again.

Pushing back my chair, I stood up.

There was only one way to figure out what was really going on here.

I had to look around. See what I could see.

Going around the desk, I walked across the room, following the way the girl had gone, to the door.

Either there had been a power outage, I was dreaming, or I was in the past.

Going down the hallway, I reached the foyer and stopped.

A bolt of lightning flashed through the window, quickly followed by another rumble of thunder.

I couldn't see the grandfather clock, but I could hear it as it steadily ticked away the minutes.

I tried to remember if I had ever heard this clock working before. I didn't think so.

It had been broken for as long as I could remember.

But it was most certainly working now.

I walked to the parlor door and looked inside. I couldn't see a damn thing.

Maybe this had not been the best idea.

I didn't have my phone with me. No flashlight of any kind.

Putting a hand against the parlor door casing, I closed my eyes.

"Can I be of assistance, Sir?"

I nearly jumped right out of my skin.

Whoever the man was, he had light.

"Yes," I said. "I…"

The man held the candle out to the side so I could see him.

He was a tall, lean black man wearing a long white cotton gown.

"I didn't mean to startle you," he said. "but I heard a noise."

"The thunder," I said, running a hand absently through my hair.

"I don't know you," the man said.

"Likewise," I said with a small smile as it occurred to me that was no longer surprised to have strange people walking around my grandfather's house in the middle of the night.

"My name is Villars," the man said. "I'm the butler."

"My name is Cameron Becquerel," I said. "I think I'm from the future."

16

ISABELLA

"I need to talk to you," I said. "about something."

I sat in a white wooden rocking chair on my brother's veranda. He sat next to me in an identical chair. He'd built both of them himself.

He'd built the house, too, with help, of course. It was a smaller version of the main Becquerel house, just much much newer.

It was a beautiful May morning early enough that dew was still on the ground. The mournful sound of a steamboat drifted through the air from the river.

I lifted the mug of hot black coffee my brother had handed me a few minutes ago and took a small sip. It was bitter and I hated the taste, but it woke my senses and that I liked.

I'd walked over to my brother's house early, specifically because I knew he got up earlier than his new wife, Sophia.

"What do you need to talk to me about?" he asked, sipping from his own coffee mug.

"Have you ever met a man named Cameron Becquerel?" I asked, holding my breath as I waited for his answer.

"No. I don't think so," he said with a little shrug. "Why?"

"Have you ever heard of him?" I persisted, not answering his question.

"No," Nathan asked again. "Why?"

"I talked to him at the party," I said. It was far from a lie, but very misleading. I wasn't ready to tell my brother everything. Not just yet.

Maybe not ever.

"Ah," Nathan said. "I see."

I rolled my eyes. "No. You don't see." But I thought maybe he actually saw more than I was ready to admit even to myself.

"What's he like?" Nathan asked.

"I don't know." I shrugged and hid behind my mug. "Nice."

"Nice?"

"I only talk to him for a moment," I said. "but he's a Becquerel I thought maybe you had heard of him. Since I hadn't."

"So you walked all the way over here just to ask me if I knew someone you met the other night?"

"Don't be mean," I said. "I was out walking anyway."

My brother looked at me sideways. He knew I didn't get up early to go walking.

But things could change. He had. He'd moved out and gotten married.

That was something I'd never expected him to do.

"I'm not being mean," he said. "It's just I've known you your whole life and never once have you shown any interest in a man."

The heat of a blush warmed my cheeks.

"I didn't say I was interested," I said. "I am merely curious. About our cousins," I added as an afterthought.

"It's okay," Nathan said. "It was bound to happen. And it's not a bad thing."

"Anyway," I said. "he asked me a strange question."

Cameron's question had caused me a sleepless night and I

figured either Nathan or Sophia would be the ones most likely to have an explanation.

I didn't have a reason for thinking that. I was merely going with my gut.

"What did he ask you?" Nathan asked, the humor in his voice turned to wariness now.

I looked away from him. Toward the river. I wavered. Maybe I didn't need to ask him after all. He was making me nervous and I hadn't even told him yet.

"If you don't tell me," Nathan said. "I can't help you."

I turned my gaze back to my brother's. He was right, of course.

I may as well ask him. I'd come all this way, after all. And he knew it.

"He asked me what year it was."

Nathan wobbled his mug in his hands, nearly dropping it.

"Are you certain?" he asked.

"I'm not making it up," I said with an annoyed glance to hide the spurt of fear that shot through me.

Now I rather wished I had made it up.

17

CAMERON

I walked along a walking path leading toward the river. The oak trees, covered with silver moss provided a canopy of shade from the warmth of the morning sun.

Villars had led me up to the third floor of the house to what he called a spare guest room. It had a bed which was all I really needed.

"Sleep here," he'd said. "we'll talk in the morning."

It was pretty much all he'd said, actually, and when I woke this morning, Villars was no where to be seen.

So I slipped downstairs and went outside.

As soon as I stepped out the back door, any uncertainty I'd had about being in the past dissipated.

My Maserati was gone. So was Grandpa's truck as well as any sign of any vehicles at all.

There was, however, a hitching post.

The kind used for horses, not for decoration.

I was familiar with the difference.

I reached the river bank and just stood there, watching the sunrise.

A paddle wheeler floated down the far side of river. From here it looked as if there were only a couple of men standing out on its decks, watching the sun rise much as I was.

I had to reconcile myself to the idea that I was indeed in the past.

For whatever reason, however it had happened, I had gone into the past.

Just like my grandmother.

Just like my sister.

I wondered if I would see them here.

I also could not but wonder if this was what happened after a person died. Maybe they went to another time.

If so, then I had died in the other life. As had my sister.

Yet if that were the case, wouldn't a body be left behind?

Or did only certain people, those who disappeared, travel back to the past?

Between my analytical mind and my creative spirit, I searched for an explanation.

Yet I knew I wasn't going to find one.

I knew that as much as I didn't want it to be true, my grandfather's explanation about the rip in time was the most likely explanation.

I had Becquerel blood. Vaughn's blood and that meant I carried the time travel spell that had saved her life.

Did that mean that I, too, was somehow saved by going through time?

Grandpa had shown me my sister's letters. She was happily married now.

He believed that she had traveled back in time to be with her soul mate.

And now I knew that my cousin, Erika and Bradley, had also traveled back in time.

Surely we must have the most convoluted family tree in the history of family trees.

Grandpas had suggested I not try to figure any of this out.

He was right.

Even if I wanted to figure it all out, there was no way it was going to happen.

If my fate was to travel through time, I wasn't leaving a family. Except my family of origin. Grandpa and my sisters. I never saw my parents anyway.

And I didn't even mind leaving Megan behind.

At least now perhaps I would meet Isabella, the girl who had haunted me the past two nights.

Did the fact that I had traveled through time mean that I had a soul mate here in the past that I was supposed to connect with?

And if so, was that girl Isabella?

I told myself it didn't matter what she looked like.

But I knew I was lying to myself.

I came from a culture of left and right swiping. Of Facebook and Instagram where people presented their best to attract a.... suitor.

Isabella's language.

I smiled.

All in all, I had to confess.

This was going to be fun.

18

ISABELLA

I paced along the porch from one end to the other as I waited for my brother to come back outside.

He'd insisted that I needed to talk to Sophia. Right now.

I thought about just walking away.

But that was merely putting off a conversation that was going to happen anyway. Eventually.

Might as well get it over with.

I leaned against the banister of the porch, my skirt belling out behind me in the breeze.

There was a dampness in the air, more so than usual.

It was going to rain today.

A bluebird landing on the ground in front of me, pecked around for a few minutes, then finding nothing to eat, flew off.

My brother's yard was barren. No flowers yet. I wondered if Sophia was the kind of person who would plant flowers outside or if she would rather stay indoors doing needlepoint and reading.

Personally, without my mother nagging at me, I would spend most of my days doing nothing more than reading.

Sophia followed Nathan out the door.

"Good morning, Isabella," she said, taking my hands in hers and pressing her cheek against mine.

"Good morning," I said. "I hadn't intended to wake you." I shot a glance at Nathan. "But my brother insisted that I talk to you now instead of later."

"Please," she said, sitting in one of the rocking chairs and indicating for me to sit next to her. "Don't give it another thought. Now..."

She smiled, but I saw the nervousness behind it. "Start from the beginning and tell me everything. Please."

Nathan paced to the end of the porch and back, coming to lean against one of the four thick white columns, facing us.

"There really isn't much to tell," I said. "I think my brother has alarmed you for no reason."

"Probably," she said. "But that's ok. It's good to see you anyway. Have you had breakfast?"

"Not really." I shook my head.

"Nathan, sweetie," she said. "Would you bring us some toast and maybe some fruit? I'm starving."

"Of course." His brow furrowed, but he pushed off the column and went inside.

Sophia turned back to me.

"Now. Where were we?"

"It's nothing really," I said. "You may know how much I dislike parties."

"I didn't," she said. "but we're definitely in agreement on that one."

"I went to the library to hide after, at my mother's insistence, dancing with some men."

Sophia put a hand over her mouth to hide a smile, but the worry didn't leave her eyes.

"I understand completely," she said. "So there was someone there?"

"Yes." I got the sense that she wanted me to tell her

everything all at once. “I talked to him, but I didn’t actually see him.”

“Why not?”

“It was dark in the library,” I said. “And since I didn’t want anyone to find me, I didn’t light a candle.”

That seemed like a given, but I didn’t say so.

“You talked,” she said. “And he told you his name.”

“He said his name was Cameron.”

She leaned forward, searching my eyes.

I took a deep breath and told her everything. About how we’d talked.

Nathan brought out a tray with a stack of toast and two plates.

“I’ll be right back with the fruit, my love” he said, kissing his wife on the lips.

“Thanks, honey.” She said.

I felt like I’d just intruded on a most private moment. Reminded myself that they were newlyweds.

As Nathan went back inside, Sophia handed me a plate with a piece of toast.

“And he told me he was looking for his sister.”

Sophia turned a bit pale.

“His sister?”

“Yes. He told me she’d been missing for ten years.”

Sophia dropped the piece of toast she was holding.

19

CAMERON

Traffic on the river quickly picked up, at least half a dozen steamboats and as many boats carrying freight passed up and down, communicating with each other by horn.

Noticing the wind was picking up, I headed home.

By the time I got back to the main house—Grandpa's house in my time, the wind whipped the silvery moss into a frenzy.

This was turning out to be one of those stormy springs.

By the time the sun was up over the trees, it was already cloudy, dark ominous clouds gathering from the west.

Two men on horseback left the stables and galloped off toward the fields. They were going to get caught in the storm. No doubt about that.

A couple of men were outside the house, closing and securing wooden shutters. Shutters that were for more than decoration. As an architect, my sister Sophia would find that concept interesting.

I went up the steps to the back veranda and sat in one of the rocking chairs to watch the activities. Wondered if there was anything I could to help.

I needed to find Villars. Villars was the one who had helped me last night.

Since I was a stranger here, I didn't think it was a good idea to walk around inside the house.

It was quite likely that I could get myself shot.

Lightning flashed in the distance following by the rumble of thunder.

Two women, dressed long belled out dresses, wearing cloaks with hoods over their head hurried down the path I had just come from minutes earlier. A man walked with them.

They were two far away for me to see their faces, especially since they were obscured by their hoods.

The man said something, but I couldn't make out his words.

As they came closer, I began to understand some of their words.

"A terrible storm."

"Stay inside."

I sat forward. Something seemed familiar.

Instead of coming my way, they turned and walked toward the front of the house.

Standing up, I went to the far end of the porch so I could hear them better.

Just as the rain started, I heard the man say something that sent my heart racing.

"Isabella..."

Isabella. I'd found her then. In the past.

Then he said something else.

"You sound like Sophia."

Sophia. My sister.

Had I found her, too?

I started to go after them, but the rain opened up and they started to run.

With the storm crashing around me, I went inside, through the back door.

I'd intercept them this way. If my sister was here, she could vouch for me to hopefully keep me from getting shot for intruding.

And… I would get to meet Isabella in person.

A bolt of lightning flashed around me just as I stepped inside.

Then I heard The Weather Channel music coming from the television in the kitchen.

I froze.

I was not in the past anymore.

20

ISABELLA

After I'd told Sophia that Cameron was looking for his missing sister, she had excused herself and gone inside.

When Nathan came out, holding a plate of fruit, I'd just shrugged.

"She went inside," I said.

A few minutes later, Sophia came back out wearing a cloak and carrying another for me.

"Where are we going?" I'd asked.

"To the main house."

Wearing our cloaks, we'd hurried over to the main house, but we'd still gotten caught in the rain.

With our cloaks hanging up to dry, the three of us sat in the parlor. Sophia and I sat on the sofa while Nathan stood at the fireplace, propped on one elbow.

He watched his wife closely.

"There's something you two aren't telling me," I said as the storm crashed over us. I knew my brother.

Sophia leaned forward and lowered her voice.

"This is going to come as a surprise," she said.

"Okay." I shrugged. "Just tell me."

Sophia and Nathan exchanged a glance.

"I'm from the future," she said.

"The—what?" I looked from her Nathan, wearing a blank expression, and back again. "You jest."

"No," Sophia said. "I'm not jesting. Have you ever known me to jest?"

I shook my head. No. I had not. In the few times I'd ever talked to Sophia, she was one of the most serious people I'd ever met.

"How can that be?" I asked. "A person can't be from the future."

Nathan came over and sat on the arm of the couch next to Sophia.

Neither of them answered me. They just looked at me.

"Have you heard of Vaughn Becquerel?" Sophia asked.

"Of course," I said. "She's our great-grandmother."

"She was my grandmother," Sophia said.

Sophia gave me a moment to absorb that. How could the same woman be Sophia's grandmother and my great-grandmother?

"She was born in the 1700s in France and was raised by nuns. Something happened to her parents, I think." Sophia ran a hand through her hair. "I'm not really sure. But when she came of age, they sent her to America to marry a man who needed a wife."

"She knew this man?" I asked.

"No. It was some kind of arranged marriage by correspondence. Anyway, her traveling party was attacked by Indians and she was the only one who survived."

"How?" I asked.

"One of the old Indians was friendly and cast a spell to save her life. He saved her life by making a rip in time and sent her through it."

"What does that have to do with you?" I asked.

"The rip in time never healed," Sophia continued. Vaughn kept traveling back and forth through time. And she passed that gene down to her children."

"Her gene?"

"It means people of her blood," Nathan said. "Her descendants can also travel through time."

Her descendants.

"Wait," I said, looking crossways at her. "I'm also one of her descendants."

"We both are," Nathan said.

"Have you traveled through time?" I asked my brother, looking him directly in the eye.

"Not... really." Nathan looked at Sophia again.

"Not really? What does that mean?"

"It means I don't think so."

I put a palm against my forehead. This was making my head hurt.

Sophia reached out and put a hand on my arm.

"Cameron is my brother," she said.

21

CAMERON

"Good morning," Grandpa said, as I stepped through the kitchen door.

Standing at the counter, pouring a cup of coffee, he looked at me over his shoulder.

"I didn't know you were up already. Want some coffee?" he asked.

I walked over and stood in front of the television without saying anything. There was a storm in west Texas. Coming this way.

No storms here. Nothing, in fact, on the radar in the south at all.

Grandpa poured me a cup of coffee and brought them both over to the table.

"You okay?" he asked, sitting down at the table.

"I don't know." I turned around and blinked, trying to focus on him.

"Something happened," Grandpa said. "You're wearing the same thing you had on yesterday."

I glanced down. He was right. I had a regular routine. Shower. Clean clothes. Breakfast.

Then I'd go to work whether it was on site or at home.

"Yes," I said. "I think it did."

"Sit," Grandpa said, pushing a chair out with his foot.

I dropped into the chair and looked at him, my thoughts in what could only be called complete disarray.

"Where did you go?" Grandpa asked.

"1853."

"Well," Grandpa said. "Want to talk about it?"

"I'm not sure."

Grandpa nudged my mug closer.

"Drink," he said.

I picked up the mug and tasted the strong, dark coffee. He was right. It helped.

"Take your time," he said. "Do you want some toast?"

I almost laughed. I wondered how many times Grandpa had dealt with this very thing. How many times had my grandmother Vaughn or my sister Sophia come back from the past, feeling distressed and disoriented? And Grandpa was there to help them through it. To reorient and calm themselves.

I could only imagine.

"Yes," I said. "Some toast would be good."

The Weather Channel forecast came over the television. "Today will be clear across the south. Perfect spring weather. No rain in the forecast."

No rain in the forecast.

And yet. I'd just come from the rain.

I sat quietly while Grandpa made toast.

When he came back bearing two plates of toast, I ripped one piece in half and ate it.

"I think I saw Sophia," I said.

Grandpa sat back in his chair.

"That's good, right?"

I took a deep breath. Let it out slowly.

Yes. That was a good thing.

The only bad thing about going to the past was coming back to the future.

22

ISABELLA

I paced across my bedroom floor. To the door. To the window. And back again.

Emma played her annoyingly happy music on the piano.

After three hours of sitting and talking with my brother and his wife, Sophia, I'd come upstairs to take a nap.

Unfortunately, my thoughts had been so twisted I hadn't slept a wink.

Finally, I'd gotten up. Washed my face and brushed my hair.

I hadn't gone down for dinner.

Villars, bless his heart, had brought me something.

"Everything will work out," he'd said before he walked away, closing the door behind him.

It seemed like an odd thing to say. Almost like he knew what I was struggling with. He couldn't though. Could he?

The clock chimed eight times. Emma would surely be coming up to bed soon.

I don't know why I was so worried about it.

I was not going down to the study tonight.

Getting mixed up in the whole time travel thing seemed like a fruitless endeavor.

Not that I was looking for a husband, but…

I paced back to the door.

The music stopped.

Out of a new habit more than anything else, I dashed to the bed, climbed in, and pulled the blanket up to my chin.

I replayed my conversations with my brother and Sophia. Circled back around to my conversations with Cameron.

He was Sophia's brother.

From the future.

If he was anywhere nearly as handsome as Sophia was beautiful, then he would be handsome indeed.

They had said that the time travel brought soul mates together.

Like Vaughn and Nathaniel. Sophia and Nathan.

And that, I realized, was what terrified me more than anything.

I was not in the market for a husband, much less a soul mate.

The thought that I might be predestined to marry Cameron frightened me. It didn't matter that I enjoyed talking with him.

It was chilling to think that I had no control over my own destiny.

That it was already decided.

I closed my eyes and lay very still as Emma changed into her nightdress and climbed into bed.

As usual, she hummed to herself.

I rolled my eyes.

How could anyone possibly be that happy all the time?

She had no idea what all was happening in her own home.

People were traveling through time. Finding their soul mates.

And all I wanted to do was to curl up in front of the fireplace with a good book and be left alone.

But fate, it seemed, had other ideas.

I was not going downstairs.

No matter how curious I was to see if Cameron was there tonight.

I was not going downstairs.

23

CAMERON

I was edgy, but I still managed to make it through the day.

I didn't do any writing. My brain couldn't sustain that much focus.

I did call the home care agency again and set up two people to come out for interviews over the next few days.

The agency emailed over their information ahead of time. Their background checks, resumes, and references.

After printing them out, I glanced at them, then left them on the kitchen table for Grandpa to take a look at. I might study them more carefully in the morning, but I was relying on the agency and Grandpa's preferences for the most part.

Other than that, I did physical chores.

I chopped firewood for Grandpa. He might not need it now, but he could use it this winter.

Even though it could have waited another week, I got the riding mower out and made a run around the yard.

I cooked dinner for us and watched a little television with Grandpa.

We did not talk about the time travel.

Things almost seemed normal. Like nothing unusual had happened. Like my sister had not traveled through time.

Like I had not traveled through time.

I had about a million questions, but I couldn't even verbalize them yet. My brain was still trying to make sense of it.

Not that it was possible to make sense of any of it.

After Grandpa went up to bed and I was feeling a bit more relaxed, I went back into the study and pulled the photographs out of the trunk again.

I went straight to the one of the beautiful young lady. Pulled it out and propped it against the desk lamp.

Maybe this was a photograph of Isabella.

I longed to know what she really looked like. To see her.

But even more than that, I longed to talk with her again.

I somehow felt like my going back in time had upset the balance of things.

By eleven o'clock I knew she wasn't coming.

I flipped open my computer, pulled up the screenplay I'd been working on and started writing.

It was as though the words just spilled out me.

If writing always came this easy I'd have more jobs than I knew what to do with.

At midnight, I saved my work and finished off a bottle of water.

Getting up, I walked to the kitchen for a refill.

The house was quiet, but it still breathed. I noticed the little things. Like the hum of the air conditioning. The click of the refrigerator as it turned on and off. A vehicle with a loud motor passing by on the River Road.

Tomorrow I would talk to Grandpa.

I needed to know if anything about the time travel was controllable.

If it was all just random, I needed to know that, too.

He had definitely been around it enough to know.

With a fresh bottle of water, I went back to the desk and just sat looking at the picture of the girl.

Classically beautiful features. High cheek bones. Long lashes.

I was falling in love with a photograph and the voice I'd heard in darkness that I'd paired with it.

24

ISABELLA

The next day I sat in the parlor with Momma again, doing needlepoint. It was a clear day with temperatures rising, but not yet unbearable. The men were out in the fields doing whatever it was that men did.

I suppose they said the same thing about us. In the parlor. Doing whatever it was that women did.

The steady ticking of the grandfather clock echoed through the house. It didn't bother me. In fact, I took comfort from it.

Emma had gone up for a nap, thankfully, instead of gracing us with her happy, happy music.

"Wear your new green dress tonight," Momma said. "It brings out the green in your eyes."

"Why?" I asked, stabbing at the cloth with my needle.

"Did you forget?" she asked. "Theodore is coming to dinner."

"Of course not," I said, picking up a different shade of green than the one I was using and held them up together.

I had absolutely forgotten.

And spending an evening with Theodore… or any other man sounded like torture.

If I was going to spend an evening with any man, I wanted it to be Cameron.

My fingers froze as my conscious brain heard what my unconscious brain was thinking.

I didn't want to spend an evening with any man.

Courtship seemed so tedious.

Momma had taught me so many things that, fortunately came second nature to me anyway. Like keeping my gaze down and looking up at a man from beneath my lashes.

But doing those things on purpose. Like trying to remember how to hold my parasol. Carrying it over the right shoulder meant you can speak to me. Carrying it closed in the right hand by the side meant follow me.

Goodness. Just say the words already.

But I was not like most women. Most women delighted in the subtleties… the challenges of flirting.

I couldn't imagine ever feeling that way.

"I'll do your hair," Momma said.

It would take two hours for me to bathe, get dressed, and have Momma do my hair.

It seemed like far too much work to do just to have dinner with a man I wasn't even interested in.

Perhaps, I thought as I threaded a needle with a new shade of green thread, I should take advantage of all the primping and go to the library after everyone went to bed, perhaps to see Cameron again.

"Nonsense," I mumbled under my breath.

"What is it, Dear?" Momma said.

"Nothing Momma," I said with a little smile. "Everything is good."

Momma would never understand. Sometimes I felt sorry for her. She'd had three sons and only one daughter and that daughter didn't particularly enjoy all the feminine things that Momma wanted to teach me.

She should have had a daughter like Emma. Emma, even at a year younger than I was, loved to dress up, and already, I'd noticed her subtle flirting with men at the balls.

Yes. Emma would have been a much better daughter for Momma.

And I was going to be poor company, indeed, for the hapless Theodore.

And if he was coming to court me, he would be sorely disappointed.

I couldn't think about much of anything other than Cameron.

And yet I'd never even actually met him. Or even seen him, for that matter.

25

CAMERON

The next few days blurred together and I did mostly the same things.

Breakfast. Work outside. Shower.

Then after lunch, I settled down at my computer and worked on my screenplay.

I spent some time on the phone with the movie director in Memphis, but the issues we discussed were minor and easily resolved.

One of the interviewees from the caregiving agency came out to talk with us. She was a middle-aged woman who seemed nice enough. Qualified of course. I wasn't sure she was a good match for Grandpa, but he seemed to think she was okay.

I had a feeling, he wasn't putting very much energy into the search. As long as I was there, he seemed content.

Tonight, after our television program, Grandpa didn't go upstairs right away like he usually did.

"I'm going to have a glass of wine," he said. "would you like one?"

"Sure." Grandpa was breaking our pattern. I liked patterns.

Patterns kept me productive and kept me from dwelling on things I couldn't understand.

A few minutes later, Grandpa held up his glass of wine in a toast.

"To time," he said.

Grandpa was not only breaking our pattern, he was bringing up the thing that I both most wanted to talk about and at the same time least wanted to talk about.

"Have you thought any more about your experience with time travel?" he asked.

"Some," I said. *All the time.*

"I'm assuming since you haven't said anything," he said. "that you haven't experienced it again."

"I'd tell you," I said.

Grandpa nodded. "We need to figure out what to do about Sophia."

I knew what he meant. It was time to tell my siblings about the time travel. It could stay an open case with local law enforcement, but the family deserved to know.

"I know," I said. "I'll set it up tomorrow. Have them come out. Maybe this weekend. Maybe the next."

"You don't seem to be in any hurry," Grandpa pointed out.

"Of course not," I said. "It makes it all so final."

"I'm not talking about your sister," Grandpa said, swirling his wine in his glass. "I'm talking about you going back to work."

I didn't say anything.

"You are going back to work at some point, right?"

I drained my glass.

"Are you kicking me out?" I asked.

Grandpa laughed. "Not at all. I'm just curious what you're thinking. You've never stayed here more than a few days and now you seem content to be here indefinitely."

"I guess so," I said, reaching for the bottle of wine and refilling my glass.

"It's not just about Sophia," I said.

Grandpa met my gaze and nodded sagely.

"I suspected as much," he said. "I noticed you haven't been talking to Megan."

Leave it to Grandpa to notice. He believed in the time travel spell down to his core. All of it. Including the part about the soul mates.

And I was beginning to think he was right about it.

26

ISABELLA

After a dinner that went much more smoothly than I could have expected, we adjourned to the parlor.

Theodore was actually a pleasant enough man. We seemed to have some things in common. I learned that he was an attorney, and as such, was well read in classic literature.

I picked up, however, on a slight snobbishness when I mentioned that I liked to read penny dreadfuls when I could get them.

Although two of my brothers were there—Nathan, of course, was not—as well as my parents and cousin, I somehow ended up seated on the sofa next to him.

Emma was preparing to sit at the piano and play something dreadfully happy.

When she stepped out of the room, I leaned over toward Momma who sat in a chair near me.

"Momma?" I said. "Do you think it might be appropriate for me play something on the piano?"

Momma's face brightened. Although I was quite proficient at playing the piano, I had not played since we'd moved here last month.

"I think that would be absolutely delightful," she said. "Go ahead."

Eager to put some distance between myself and Theodore, I hopped up and went to sit at the piano.

Settling in, I ignored Emma's obvious surprise and ill-concealed disappointment when she came back into the parlor and found me sitting at the piano.

Lightly touching the keys, I decided to play one of my favorite pieces, even though I was certain, although they wouldn't say it, that it wasn't very popular with most people.

I started slowly, allowing my fingers to become acquainted with the keys.

Then I settled into the music, letting my fingers fly over the keys as the grandfather clock began to chime the hour.

The chimes seemed to blend perfectly with my music.

I lifted my head, closed my eyes, and lost myself in the soulfully, heart-wrenchingly sad music.

Everything else faded into the background.

I didn't fight it when my thoughts zeroed in and settled on Cameron.

I didn't know how I could be so enchanted with a man I had never even laid eyes on, but I decided in that moment not to fight it.

If I saw him again, that is.

If I saw him again, I vowed to myself, I would be bold, go against convention and actually see him.

Conventions, I decided were for the faint of heart.

Besides, a man coming from the future may not have the same expectations as men like Theodore had.

Perhaps a man from the future would be willing to discuss modern literature.

I brought myself back to reality as I finished the piece and looked around the room.

Theodore was speaking with Andrew and apparently they found something mutually amusing.

As the last strains of the music faded away, I stood up from the piano and darted from the room.

I had completed my obligations. I had been charming and sufficiently demure.

As far as I was concerned, nothing else was required of me for the evening.

After leaving the parlor without a word and, probably without being noticed, I put one foot on the stairs, then stopped.

I didn't want to go upstairs to my bedroom.

27

CAMERON

My fingers stilled on the keyboard and I looked up at the photograph of the girl I'd begun calling Isabella. It didn't matter that I didn't really know who the girl was. To me she was Isabella.

If and when I learned differently, I would adapt my way of thinking.

As I stared at her beautiful coiffed hair, the strains of a soulfully sad song started low, then became louder.

My imagination was becoming much more vivid these days. Since the overhead light was on as well as the lamp on my desk, I knew I was still in the present. In my own time.

Yet, I was hearing hauntingly beautiful piano music as it drifted through the house.

The music settled over me, like a calming balm, and I went back to writing. I took my time, channeling my muse onto the screen through my fingers.

Pausing, I looked up at Isabella's black and white photograph.

The grandfather clock began to chime the hour.

I tapped a couple of words.

The grandfather clock.

The broken grandfather clock.

I slowly closed the lid of my Macbook and sat back, taking in my surroundings.

The music had stopped.

My fingers rested on the cool aluminum of the computer.

The electric lights shone brightly.

Everything seemed to be normal. Except for the clock.

As the last chime hung in the air... I hadn't counted them... I sat very still.

Then I looked up from the black and white photograph to the very real, very colorful version of the girl.

She wore her hair exactly the same as the photograph, but now I could see that she had beautiful emerald green eyes framed by thick dark lashes and plump pink lips that begged to be kissed.

Her long dress in shades of green accentuated the green in her eyes, making them even more vibrant.

I didn't dare blink for fear that she would vanish.

Perhaps I imagined it, but the girl in the photograph had come to life.

I was still firmly in the present, yet a girl from the past stood firmly in front of me.

It hadn't happened as I'd expected, but my wish had come true.

Isabella stood in front of me.

Unless...

"Are you Isabella?" I asked.

"Yes," she said and I immediately recognized her voice from the two nights we had spoken in this very room. "Are you Cameron?"

"Yes. How are you here?" I asked. "Are you real?"

She smiled a little. "I don't know. And as far as I know."

She watched me as I walked around from the desk to stand

in front of her. I was a full head taller than she was, so she tilted her head to keep her eyes locked on mine.

"Come," I said. "Sit with me." I swept a hand toward the loveseat on the other side of the room.

Her long skirts swished as she turned and, deftly maneuvering the belled out skirts, she walked in front of me and ever so gracefully sat down.

Her intoxicating scent followed her. Like magnolia blooms and sunshine.

She swept her skirts aside for me to sit next to her.

Seated, I studied her like an artist would study a work of art.

She blushed and looked away.

"May I touch your hand?" I asked.

28

ISABELLA

"You want to know if I'm real," I said, looking into Cameron's sky-blue eyes.

I had been right in predicting that he was handsome. Clean shaven with some evening stubble over his chiseled jaw.

He had a kind demeanor and the way he looked at me made me a little weak in the knees.

The air felt different. Cooler. And the room was lit up like daytime, yet it was dark outside. The house was quiet. I didn't hear the clock or my family's voices. Certainly no music and as I was leaving the room, Emma was already up, heading to the piano to play her overly happy music.

I was not in my time.

"Yes," he said.

Did he know I was from the past? It wasn't likely. How could he possibly know? I wouldn't have known if my own brother had not married a woman from the future.

He immediately took my right hand as I held it out. His gentle touch sent an array of emotions through me.

He didn't just *touch* my hand, he *held* my hand.

My breath hitched. Then he was holding both my hands with his and gazing into my eyes.

I struggled to gather my scattered thoughts.

"Do you think I'm real?" I asked, my voice barely audible.

He brought my hands to his lips. Kissed the back of one. Then the other.

"I'm pretty sure you are," he said. "Can you stay?"

"Can I…?" Could I? Did I want to? I looked down, unable to continue looking at him.

He must have sensed my sudden confusion and emotional tumult.

He released my hands, but he didn't look away.

"Say you'll stay," he said, with a little smile.

I stood up, then turned back to face him.

"How can I promise to stay when I don't even know where I am?"

He looked crestfallen. I'd disappointed him.

"You're with me," he said. "Does it really matter?"

"Of course it matters," I said. But did it?

Standing up, he stood in front of me, taking my hands again. He lightly swept a thumb over my cheek and I swayed forward, closing my eyes.

He kissed me on the forehead.

Then I blinked, opening my eyes again.

We gazed into each other's eyes as the clock began to chime the hour.

The clock.

I gasped and looked over my shoulder.

Then I heard my cousin's happy piano music coming from behind me. Soft at first, then louder.

I felt Cameron's hands in mine, but I didn't feel like I was actually with him.

I felt like I was slipping away.

I turned back to him, but he was hazy now. It was like he was in some kind of misty fog.

Looking down at our clasped hands, I held tighter.

He looked startled.

Then I blinked and he was gone.

I was standing in the shadows of the library. Alone.

I went to the armchair and dropped into it. The house was quiet now. Like everything had suddenly been turned off. The only sound came from the steady ticking of the grandfather clock.

I'd been in the future. I'd met Cameron Becquerel.

He'd asked me to stay and I'd wanted to stay, but I couldn't. Not even with him holding my hands.

"Isabella," Father said, coming to the door holding up a lantern. "Where have you been?"

"Right here," I said, though I had just been asking myself the same thing. "Just sitting here."

"No," Father said. "We've been searching for you for hours. I looked in here myself."

I put a hand over my eyes.

"Father," I said. "I don't know what's happening."

29

CAMERON

As the echo of the twelfth chime of the grandfather clock faded away, I stood in front of my desk, staring into space—the space where Isabella had just been.

I could still smell her. Magnolia blooms and sunshine.

I could still feel her hands on mine.

She had been here.

And I had watched her fade away right in front of me.

Grandpa had not said anything about this to me.

He also had not seemed to think that Isabella would be traveling to the future. He had not said anything about more than one person traveling through time.

I needed to find him. To ask him.

Leaving the room, I dashed out of the library and made it as far as the foyer when my phone chimed with a text.

MEGAN: *Hi Sweetie. Guess what?*

Megan. How could she have such timing?

I was about to put the phone away without answering.

MEGAN: *I'm driving down your grandfather's driveway.*

Holding my phone out, I stared at it. Unable to think.

No. Instead of going upstairs, I went to the front door and looked outside.

The headlights of a car were indeed coming down the driveway.

Megan could NOT be coming here. This was not okay. How did she even find me?

And why now? Why was she here just minutes after I'd held Isabella's hands in mine?

Why was Megan here just minutes after I'd been with the woman I was in love with?

Startled by my thoughts, I checked the time. It was eight o'clock.

The clock had chimed twelve times.

Midnight.

Isabella had been with me at Midnight.

But now it was only nine o'clock.

Our time was out of sync.

I laughed at the thought.

That was an understatement.

Something was happening. The present and the past seemed to be merging.

No. That wasn't possible. That was the creative writer in me.

The present and past could not merge into one space.

Could it?

I'd been in the present, but I'd heard the grandfather clock —the broken clock—chime twelve times just as Isabella had faded away.

Back into the past. She'd gone back into the past. I was certain of it.

But why?

Why had she come forward in time? And just for a brief moment? Just long enough for me to see her. To smell her. To feel her hands in mine.

And why on earth would Megan be driving down my driveway?

Megan's timing was unspeakably bad.

I did not want to see her right now. To be truthful, I didn't want to see anyone other than Isabella.

But I had no choice. I'd been needing to deal with this situation anyway.

I'd been putting it off because I hadn't been sure what I was going to do.

But I knew now.

I knew what I had to do.

As I went to open the door and step out onto the veranda to greet Megan, it occurred to me that maybe that was why Isabella had paid me a visit in my time.

30

ISABELLA

I sat in the parlor, with a blanket over my shoulders, a hot mug of tea in my hands.

I sat with Father, Sophia, and Nathan.

Everyone else had gone back to bed as soon as they heard I had been found safe and sound. Theodore had left shortly after dinner before my family had begun to look for me.

Apparently, I had gone missing for at least four hours. Maybe longer, since I wasn't missed at first.

My family was used to me disappearing off to myself for hours at the time.

"Tell us again," Sophia said. "Please."

I understood Sophia wanted to know details. I had been with her brother Cameron.

"I escaped the dinner party," I said with an apologetic glance at Father. "and I went to the library."

"And the room was bright?" Sophia asked.

"Not at first," I said, replaying the events of the evening in my head. For me, it had been less than hour, so my memory was fresh.

"It was dark when I stepped into the room. Then it slowly brightened. Like stepping outside into the sunshine."

Sophia nodded.

"Is that normal?" Nathan asked.

"Yes," Sophia told him. "It's the electricity."

Nathan nodded. Apparently that meant something to him. Something they had discussed.

With the three of them watching me, I continued.

"As I walked into the room, I saw a man sitting behind the desk. The desk isn't there now. But I knew it was Cameron. I don't know how I knew. Maybe because that was where I'd seen… rather heard… him before."

"How did he look?" Sophia asked.

Unable to help myself, I smiled.

"He looked well." *So handsome. The most handsome man I've ever seen.*

Sophia nodded and blew out a breath of relief.

"And then you just talked?" Nathan asked.

"Yes." Then because it seemed like it might actually be important, I told them more. "He wanted to know if I was real, so he touched my hands."

He held my hands. But I wanted to keep that to myself for the moment.

"That sounds like him," Sophia said, with a smile.

"You miss him, don't you?" Nathan asked her.

"Of course," she said. "Just as you would miss Sophia.

Father had been listening quietly.

"There's a reason this happened," he said. "Time travel does not just happen for no reason."

My heart skittered.

He was talking about fate.

"Isabella," he said. "I know you don't want to marry. At least not right now. But we need to consider that he might be the one for you."

Sophia placed a hand on Nathan's arm.

"Oh my God," she said. "You're right. You and my brother are soul mates."

"Wait," Nathan said. "we don't know that."

But as Sophia and I looked at each other, we both knew that it could be true.

And now that I'd met Cameron, the whole idea was growing on me.

31

CAMERON

I'd tried to get Megan to sit with me in the parlor, but that wasn't her style.

She insisted on seeing the house. At least the first floor.

Holding my hand, pulling me along as she wandered, she didn't even notice that I was being distant.

"It's so… old," she said as we crossed the foyer.

"Of course it is," I said. "but it's solid."

To her credit, she kept further thoughts about the age of the house to herself.

I bristled as she stepped into the study.

Even though I was technically Grandpa's study, he didn't use it, and I considered it my personal space.

It was especially personal because this was where I had met Isabella. Where I had talked to her. Where I had held her hands.

Releasing my hand, she went over to my desk.

"Always working." She lifted the lid of my computer. "What are you working on?"

"Just playing around with an idea," I said.

She nodded and closed the lid. I'd noticed that if my writing didn't involve her, she had little interest in it.

"Who's this?" she asked, picking up Isabella's black and white photograph."

"Careful," I said, gently snatching the photograph from her hand. "It's very old."

"And she's very pretty."

"She lived a long time ago, Megan," I said.

"So she's your inspiration."

Without answering, I set the photograph back down.

"What's her name?" Megan asked.

"I really don't know," I said. "There's nothing written on the back."

Was Megan seriously jealous of Isabella? Under other circumstances, I might have found it kinda sweet.

But not now. Not when Megan actually had a good reason to be jealous of Isabella.

"What do you call her in your work?" Megan asked.

"Seriously?" I asked, becoming exasperated now. "You know I don't share my work until it's finished."

"Right," she said, whirling around and going to sit on the loveseat where Isabella had sat only minutes earlier.

Seeing her sitting there honestly made me feel a little bit ill.

She patted the loveseat.

I shook my head.

"Come," she said with a little pout. "Come sit by me."

"No," I said. "This is where I work. You know I don't like anyone in my office space."

"Right," she said. "How could I forget?"

She got up and, still pouting, went back to the parlor.

Now whenever I thought about meeting Isabella in the study, I'd have an image of Megan sitting there, too.

Damn it, Megan.

Just happy to have her away from the study, I followed.

"What are you doing here?" she asked.

"I came to see you," she said. "I was having trouble focusing without you there."

I seriously doubted that, but I could believe that she missed having me there as part of her audience.

"I'm sure you did just fine," I said, going to the liquor cabinet to pour myself a glass of wine. "You want some?" I asked, indicating the bottle as I uncorked it.

"No," she said.

I'd never known Megan to turn down a drink, especially not a glass of wine.

Swirling the glass of wine, I stood and watched her.

"Something's different," she said.

"You show up here in the middle of the night with no warning. So, yes. Something is different."

"I thought you'd be happy to see me," she said.

I came from the philosophy of pulling the band-aid off quickly. It was the way I wanted to be treated, so I did the same.

"Actually, being here has given me a lot of time to think," I said. "And I don't think we need to see each other anymore."

Megan was speechless for all of about five seconds.

"I see," she said. "And you were going to tell me this when?"

"I was going to tell you when I got back. After I decided."

"So you already knew?"

"Come on, Megan," I said. "Don't make this more difficult than it has to be. You can sleep here tonight."

As much as I didn't want her here, it was the right thing to do. I could not ask her to drive back alone, late at night.

She stood up and, coming to stand in front of me, glared into my eyes.

"You couldn't make me spend the night under the same roof as you even if I had to walk all the way back to Memphis."

She picked up her handbag as she walked toward the door.

"Oh," she said, stopping to turn back to me. "Don't bother coming back to the set. I'm the director now and you're fired."

Well, I thought, you learn something new every day. I had not known that Megan was a bad breaker-upper.

I listened to her slam her car door, then listened as the car traveled away down the dirt road.

I refilled my glass of wine and sat down on the sofa.

I had some work to do. I had to purge Megan out of my head so I could replay meeting Isabella.

That's what I got, I guess, for not breaking up with Megan when I first figured out when I was going to.

The problem was, I wasn't quite sure when that had been.

Maybe it had been that first night when I'd first talked to Isabella.

32

ISABELLA

Father, of course, told Momma about the whole time-travel thing. I didn't want anyone making a big deal about it, but I was not surprised that he told her. They told each other everything.

It would have been okay with me, except that now Momma watched me like a hawk.

We sat together on the sofa in the parlor two days later, both working on our respective needlework.

"Isabella," she said, her hands idle in her lap. "You should have told me when this thing first started."

"There was nothing to tell," I said, stabbing at the cloth in my hand with the little needle.

"Okay," she said, picking up her needle again. "I can believe that."

"Momma," I said, setting my own embroidery hoop down. "Did you ever travel through time?"

"No," she said, keeping her gaze on the work in her hands.

"Do you think it was because Father was already living in the same time as you?"

Momma blew out a breath and set her needlework down. I shifted beneath her penetrating gaze, but didn't look away.

"Yes," she said. "Did anything else happen in the library?"

"What? No." I looked away, feeling the heat on my cheeks.

I couldn't tell her how I'd felt when he held my hands. I couldn't explain that. Nor could I explain the way it had made me feel when he'd kissed me on my forehead.

But the worst of it was the heartbreak at leaving him.

"You love him," Momma said.

"No," I said. "Maybe. I don't know."

"You will," Momma said. "You'll figure it out."

There was something in her voice that I didn't like. I wasn't sure what it was, but it sounded a lot like disappointment.

"Please don't worry, Momma," I said. "You know I've never been impulsive."

"You're right," Momma said. "But Isabella. I've never known you to be interested in a man either."

"Is it so bad, Momma?" I asked before picked up my basket of thread.

"Is what so bad?" she asked.

"Is it so bad that I like Cameron? You seem like you're mad at me for liking him."

"I'm not mad," she said, putting a hand on my wrist. "I'm just worried. I'm worried that you'll go through time and I'll never see you again."

"I guess it's possible," I said, knowing it wasn't what Momma want to hear.

Cameron was all I could think about.

The way he looked. The way he looked at me.

It was all so new to me.

I'd fallen hard and fast for him.

And I knew that I would go anywhere to be with him even if it meant going to another time and leaving my family behind.

I did not want to, but if it meant being with Cameron, then I would do it.

I would leave behind a world I knew… my own people.

33

CAMERON

Over the next week, I broke my pattern. Instead of getting up and showering first thing, I put on my running shoes and went outside for a run.

I hadn't had much exercise since I'd gotten here and I was starting to feel it in my muscles.

I stuck to the trails today, winding my way along toward the river.

The oak trees stood guard above me, their silver moss waving like flags to spur me on.

I reached the river and noted just how different it looked now from in the past.

Instead of the elegant looking steamboats, there were mostly ugly rusty looking tugboats piled high with freight.

The closer I got to the river, the more it smelled like decaying animal flesh.

I veered away from the river toward my father's construction site. Knowing him, he'd probably just let it sit there and decay until it rotted back into the earth.

Maybe I'd hire someone to come out and clean it up. Just another thing to put on my list of things I was responsible for.

Something was seriously wrong with either me or my family for putting everything on my shoulders.

Maybe it was my fault for taking on too much.

Besides setting up someone to clean up this mess, another caregiver was coming out to interview today. The sooner I could get that set up, the better.

I had to contact my sister, Mackenzie and Victoria to come out here so I could tell them that our other sister, Sophia, had gone back in time so we could stop looking for her to either come home or show up dead somewhere.

And apparently, I was now out of work, so I had to figure out what to do about that.

I shouldn't have trouble getting more work. It was possible that Megan could try to blackball me, but she did not have the best reputation in the industry and besides that, once people knew we'd dated, they would understand. Nothing like a woman scorned.

It might in fact, get me some sympathy at least from my male colleagues.

However.

And this was a big however.

My shoes pounded along the hard-packed earth, sending squirrels scampering and birds fluttering. I wasn't just upsetting my pattern, I was upsetting the whole pattern of wildlife by being out here.

I wasn't sure if I wanted to look for more work in the industry.

I had found my sister.

And there were playwrights in the 1800s. A playwright was close enough to a scriptwriter to count.

And, the most important thing was that Isabella was in the past.

If it was possible that I could go back in time and stay

there… with Isabella… then if given a choice, that was what I wanted to do.

I had a lot of things to do here, yet, but overall, I was clearing my list. Actually my list was being cleared for me.

I never would have suspected that Megan would become director and fire me.

Somewhere in the back of my mind, I'd been trying to figure out how to resign.

Grandpa had called me on that one when he'd asked me if I ever intended to go back to work.

I guess the short answer was no. Not really.

I stopped at the construction site and walked through what had been the framework of a house. Father had been building a replica of the main house to live in himself and my sister, an architect, had been helping him.

When she'd gone missing, my father—who rarely showed any kind of emotion at all—had decided that he did not want to live here after all. Maybe, for him, that was an emotional decision.

From what I could gather, Father's new wife was relieved. Not too many people, especially women, wanted to come out here to live in the country like this.

It wasn't something most women would choose to do on purpose.

I wondered if Sophia had given any thought to leaving her work behind. According to her letters, she was happy in the past.

A mother.

A car with a loud muffler went down the highway.

There was actually a lot of work for a writer in the 1800s. It was the days of Penny Dreadfuls and dime novels. I wasn't sure on the actual publication dates on the two. Maybe that was something I should go ahead and research. Anything I could find out ahead of time would put me that much more ahead of the game.

I'd never actually written a novel, but I'd written a lot of screenplays. Maybe I could turn my screenplay writing skills into novel writing skills.

It would not be a far reach.

It was funny how my thoughts so easily flowed to picturing me in the past.

I reached the main house. Ran up the steps to the veranda at the back of the house, then stopped and did a few stretches.

As soon as I stepped through the back door, I could smell the coffee Grandpa had brewing.

I went into the kitchen where Grandpa sat at the table, buried behind a newspaper.

He lowered it when I stepped inside.

"Out running again?" he asked.

"Lots of things to sort through," I said.

"I guess so," Grandpa said, setting the newspaper aside. "What Megan did must have come as quite a shock, I'd think."

"Yes," I said. "Caught me off guard." Though Megan wasn't what I wanted to think about.

"You want to talk about it?"

"Not really." I got up to make myself some toast. Not because I necessarily wanted it, but because I needed something to do. To distract myself.

"You want some toast?" I asked Grandpa.

"Sounds good."

I popped four pieces of toast into the toaster and stared out the window at the wind blowing through the oak trees.

Stormy. Again. I liked stormy.

"What time is that girl coming out to interview?"

"Two o'clock. I think."

The toast popped up and I put two pieces on one plate and

two on another. Got out some butter out of the refrigerator and some strawberry jam for Grandpa.

I slid into my chair and buttered a slice of toast. Handed Grandpa the knife.

I sat back in my chair and watched Grandpa spread jam over his toast.

"Grandpa?"

Grandpa looked up. Took a bite of toast. Waited for me to continue.

"Do you know how to get me back in time?"

"Sort of," Grandpa said, with what I swear was a little smile. "There's a key in the clock face keyhole now."

"What does that mean?" My heart rate shot into overdrive.

"It wasn't there before," Grandpa said.

"Before?"

"Before your sister went back in time."

"Can the key get me back in time?" I asked.

"I think so," Grandpa said, sipping his coffee. "Maybe."

"Then it is possible?"

"Sophia did it," Grandpa said with a little shrug.

That was it. My sister held the answers.

There was only one problem. A very big problem.

I had no way of communicating with my sister.

The secret had gone into the past with her.

34

ISABELLA

"You have to go," Father said.

I sat with Mother on the sofa in the parlor.

We'd had a pleasantly quiet afternoon when Father came in.

He paced in front of us. His expression even more serious than usual.

"I'm not going," I insisted, looking to Mother for support, but she refused to make eye contact with me.

That meant she was siding with Father on this one.

I had no doubt they had already talked about this. They always stuck together.

"I know how you feel about marriage. That you are not ready to think about it." He glanced at Momma.

"But you will go to the ball tonight." He turned around and strode from the room.

Momma picked up her needlepoint.

It wasn't cold, but we had a fire going to ward off an unseasonable coolness.

"Momma," I said. "Why is Father so adamant about me going to the ball?"

Momma dropped her hands in her lap and met my gaze.

"He's afraid," she said.

Afraid?

"What is he afraid of?"

Momma put a hand on mine.

"He's afraid of losing you." She took a deep breath. "We both are."

She and I had already had this conversation once. About her not wanting me to travel through time.

I think she knew I would do it. That I would do whatever it took to be with him.

"Momma," I said. "Making me go the ball tonight won't stop me from loving Cameron."

"I know," she said. "But he's been here… in this time… maybe he can come here instead of you going there."

She was talking like it was just a matter of hopping on a train to go to a different time.

"It's just happens, right? There's no way to control it."

"I… no," she shook her head. You… need to talk to Sophia."

"I've already talked to her."

"I know, but I think there might be something you haven't talked about."

"Like what?"

Momma clasped her hands together in her lap and leaned forward, keeping her voice low.

"I think Sophia might know how to make the time travel happen."

"What? Why do you think that?"

"Just talk to her again," Momma said, shaking her head.

"Okay," I said. "I'll talk to her… again." I picked up my canvas.

"But Isabella?"

"Yes?" I looked at Momma.

"Tell her about Cameron."

"She knows—"

"No. Tell her how you feel about Cameron."

"But he's her brother."

"Tell her," Momma said. "If you don't, she can't help you."

35

CAMERON

I drove into town the next day. Not for any particular reason. I just needed to put the top down and drive.

It felt good to have the wind on my skin and the warm sun on my head.

I took the curves maybe a little bit faster than I should have, but I felt alive. More alive than I had in a really long time

I parked my Maserati on Main Street and it got me a lot of looks. Not too many red sports cars in downtown Natchez.

I whistled to myself as I walked along the sidewalk, not heading anywhere in particular.

It was a little odd, walking by myself and without a purpose.

I was usually either working or going somewhere specific or I was with someone. Lately that someone was usually Megan.

I was good for me to get away by myself. Without her. Without anyone.

It allowed me to do a kind of reset. To remember who I was.

I was not a Hollywood prima donna. At my core, I was basically a simple man. With basic needs.

I needed a good place to live. A computer to write on.

And I wanted a family.

The thought came unexpected and unbidden.

I'd been caught in my career over the past few years and I hadn't given much thought to anything other than work.

But being with Grandpa these weeks… basically living with him… had given me a new perspective on what was important in life.

He'd had Vaughn, my grandmother, and they had a good life together. I could see that Grandpa had no regrets.

I didn't want to have any regrets.

A store, aptly named *The Haberdashery,* looked interesting, so I stepped inside. The store, cool inside, was empty. Apparently shopping for hats was not a very popular pastime at the moment.

The story I was playing around with was set partly in the 1800s, so I was curious enough to try on some different styles of hats.

This one definitely had a variety.

I didn't see anyone behind the counter or on the floor, so I took the opportunity to try on some of the hats.

First, I tried on a fedora. Checked myself out in the mirror. It wasn't half bad.

I put it back on the shelf and picked up a black top hat.

For some reason, it made me smile.

I set it on my head and immediately stood a little taller.

There was something about a top hat that made a man stand out from the others.

I decided to wear the top hat around while I was in the store. To get a better feel for it.

I added a walking stick to my new outfit and moved along to the back of the store to browse some basic shirts.

A young woman came out from the back.

She stood behind the counter watching me with a little smile.

"That suits you," she said. The woman had a bit a French accent that I found endearing.

"You think?" I doffed the hat, feeling quite dashing.

"I do think so," she said, coming out from behind the counter.

The woman was petite. Dark hair. Smoky eyes.

"You'll need one of these," she said. Handing me what looked like a white scarf.

"Thank you," I said, taking the silk scarf and looking dubiously at it.

"It's a cravat," she said.

"Ah." Now it made sense. "I don't have anywhere to wear it."

"You will," she said.

Now that she was closer, I noticed that her eyes were actually a deep green.

Before I had time to contemplate the vague statement, she moved on.

"Are you shopping for a particular event?" she asked or just looking around?"

"I'm just looking around," I said. "Nothing in particular."

The young lady stayed beside me as I browsed the shirts.

"I should put the hat back," I said, taking it off my head.

"No." She held up a hand. "Please don't. I like seeing you in it. Besides," she said with a little smile. "It's good for business."

I grin at her as a young couple walked in and started trying on hats.

"Maybe," I said. "It's kind of slow today."

"It's always slow," she said.

"Have you been in business long?" I asked, setting the hat back on my head.

"Seems like forever," she said with a little shrug.

"I understand." I nodded toward the couple. "Do you need to help them? I'm okay."

"They'll be alright," she said, not taking her eyes off mine.

It was oddly disconcerting and comforting at the same time.

"I think I'll take the hat," I said.

"Good choice." She smiled and held out her hand. "I'll get you a hat box."

I started to tell her I'd just wear it, but I remembered I was driving a comfortable.

I followed her to the counter.

"Do you want the walking cane and handkerchief, too?" she asked as she pulled out a flat hat box and put it together.

"Do you recommend them?" I asked. Her opinion suddenly meant a great deal.

"I do," she said, placing the hat in the box. "So much so that I'll throw in the cravat."

I handed her the cravat and she tucked it inside the box with the hat.

"Pretty soon you'll be selling me a tux," I said.

"You don't need one. At least not right now," she said. "The hat, cane, and cravat will do you just fine."

The woman, I decided as I handed her my credit card, was too good at her job. I'd come in for a hat—to try on hats—and I was leaving with not only the hat, but also a cane and a complimentary cravat thrown in.

"What are you going to do?" She asked as she created a receipt on the computer to print out.

"I don't really know," I said.

She put the hat box in a large handled paper bag, wrote something on the receipt before placing it in the bag, and came around to hand it to me.

It was a nice touch. She was good.

"Try the window," she said before she walked off, going over to help the young couple.

As I walked toward the front door, I looked to the display window, looking for an answer to what she was talking about.

The woman looked oddly familiar, but there was no way I could possibly know who she was.

Finding no obvious answers in the display window, I walked back to my car, suddenly ready to get back to Grandpa's house. I'd been gone long enough.

Having had enough of the wind, I hit a button to put the top back up.

I started the motor, but before driving off, I opened the bag and pulled out the receipt.

I fully expected to see her name. Maybe a quickly scribbled thank you.

Instead, her note read *Follow your heart.*

A rather odd statement to write on a receipt. But I supposed that any woman who had the guts to open a haberdashery in Natchez could afford a little eccentricity. It was to be expected at any rate.

The cravat was listed for almost two hundred dollars with a credit right beneath it.

That was quite a discount. I hoped she didn't get into trouble for doing it.

I turned on the radio to drown out my thoughts and headed back to Grandpa's house.

36

ISABELLA

Sophia and I sat on the balcony of her upstairs sitting room. She claimed it was her favorite room in the whole house. I could see why. She had a perfectly wonderful view of the river from here.

A steamboat, packed with women wearing long colorful dresses, floating past on the river blew its whistle, sending a mournful wail across the water. Traffic on the river was much louder here than it was at the main house. Occasionally, when the night was quiet and the wind was right, I could hear the whistles from here.

Sophia handed me a hot mug of tea. I sipped it, letting the warmth take some of the chill out of me. My chill wasn't from the weather, it came from within.

After talking with my mother, I'd walked over to Sophia and Nathan's house. I would have just enough time to spend about an hour, then I had to go back to get ready for the ball that I did not want to go to.

I was still halfway planning on finding a way out of it. Just didn't know what that was yet. Something that wouldn't cause my father undue anger.

If I had to go, I would just go. Get it over with.

"You're here to talk about the time travel," she said.

"Yes. Momma said you might know something I don't. Something that could maybe help it happen."

Sophia inhaled sharply.

"Maybe," she said, turning away to stare out the window. "But unfortunately, it won't help you."

Disappointment washed over me. More than I had expected.

"It's okay," I said.

"No." Sophia looked back at me, her eyes moist with unshed tears. "It's not okay. It's you. And my brother. You're supposed to be together. And I feel like I should be doing something to help. But I don't know what it is."

I reached out. Put a hand over.

"Please don't distress," I said. "If we're soul mates. Fate will find a way to put us together. Right?"

"Right." She took a deep breath. Looked away again. "My grandpa would know what to do. If I could just talk to him."

The grandfather clock—a replica of the one in the main house—began to chime the hour.

"I have to go," I said. "My father insists that I go to the ball tonight. As much as I don't want to go, I haven't found a way out of it."

"I understand," she said, turning back to me. "Don't give up hope. Like you said. Fate will find a way for you to get together. If it's supposed to happen."

"Do you think it will?" I asked. "Really?"

"Yes," she said. "I have faith. I never gave up hope that I'd be with Nathan. And here we are."

Before leaving, I leaned over gave her a quick hug.

"Don't worry," she said. "Have fun at the ball. No one can expect you to look for a husband. Not when we all know where your heart is."

Her words warmed my heart.

It helped that Sophia understood. Father may not agree with her sentiment, but Sophia had enough conviction for my entire family.

I could endure the ball. Just knowing that I wasn't expected to have to flirt and look for a husband, I could get through it.

37

CAMERON

Grandpa was sitting in a rocking chair on the veranda when I got back. I'd told him I was going for a drive, but hadn't said how long I'd be. I hadn't even known.

I parked and got out of the car, then grabbed my shopping bag from the passenger side.

"You weren't gone very long," Grandpa said as I took the stairs.

"Long enough,"

"You went shopping," he said.

Now I felt guilty for not taking him with me or at the least calling to see if he needed anything while I was in town. Grandpa didn't drive any, so I was feeling more than a little insensitive.

I hadn't been planning on sharing what I tried to convince myself were no more than props, but I found myself pulling my new purchases out and modeling them for him.

I draped the cravat over my neck and put the top hat on my head.

"I don't how to tie it," I said holding up the ends of the cravat.

"Come here," Grandpa said, standing up. "It's not much different from a tie."

He took the cravat, adjusted it, did an over and under, a loop, then tucked it into my shirt collar.

"There," he said, stepping back. "You look quite debonair."

"Where did you learn how to do this?" I asked.

"Your grandmother." He shrugged and sat back down.

"Right. Of course." I grabbed the cane and tucked it beneath my left arm.

"Very good."

"It would look better with a tux," I said.

"You don't need that yet," he said.

"That's what the young lady said." I froze and searched his face.

This was too bizarre. Too coincidental.

"What was her name?" Grandpa asked, looking at the name splashed across my shopping bag.

"I didn't get it," I said.

Grandpa nodded. "Did she say anything else," he asked.

I handed him the receipt.

"Follow your heart," he read aloud. "Sage advice."

"But it hardly seems relevant."

"Maybe you just have to put it all together."

"Maybe." I set the cane down, took off the hat, and sat down in the chair next to his.

It was most unsettling.

"If you get the opportunity to go back in time," Grandpa said. "You have to go. Don't worry about me."

My heart broke at the thought of leaving Grandpa here all alone.

"I still have to talk to Mackenzie and Victoria."

"I know," he said. "but I can do it if I need to."

"You're trying to run me off again," I said, teasingly.

"Not on your life," Grandpa said. "But you have to live your life. Do what's right for you."

I knew he was right. It made me sad to think about leaving Grandpa, but I knew that if I found a way back to Isabella, I would take it. I had to.

38

ISABELLA

"May I claim one of your dances?" Theodore asked as he dropped onto the chair next to mine.

I raised an eyebrow at his informal and thus inappropriate request to dance. He was supposed to stand in front of me and request the honor of a dance. But I suppose that since the party was in his parents' home, he thought the rules did not apply to him.

Another reason why I was happy I had not agreed to have him court me. Conventions were very important. And purposely disregarding them was a slap in society's face.

I lifted the dance card strapped to my wrist.

"Unfortunately," I said with a tight smile. "My dance card is full."

"That's interesting," he said. "since there have already been two dances and you didn't dance either of them."

I lowered my dance card filled with bogus names I'd invented at random and held it close.

"That seems quite impolite of you to point out."

He grinned.

"I suppose I should be content that you haven't run off yet."

"Excuse me?"

Dancers twirled around the dance floor, smaller than the one at the Becquerel house, I noted with some pride.

Both my mother and father had agreed that I was not required to dance with anyone if I didn't want to.

"You do know," Theodor said. "that the purpose of attending a ball is to dance. It's impolite to attend and not dance."

"Is it not also impolite to ask casually for a dance?"

"Then I suppose we are both equally impolite."

"You are a cad," I said.

He laughed.

"Don't worry." He stood up and bowing politely in front of me, kept his voice low. "I'm sure you'll find someone who overlooks your poor breeding."

I clamped my mouth shut to keep from further pointing out he was the one with poor breeding.

My brother, Nathan, reached my side as Theodore walked away.

His physique was similar to Cameron's, but he was so completely different.

"Is he bothering you?" Nathan asked.

"He's not worth worrying about," I said, but I was quite happy to see my brother.

Nathan sat beside me.

"What are you doing here?" I asked. My brother and Sophia rarely attended social engagements. They preferred to stay to themselves. No one faulted them for it since they were still within the realm of being newlyweds.

"Sophia wanted to speak with you."

"Where is she?" I asked, looking past him.

"She's outside in the carriage," he said. "waiting for us."

"We should go then," I said quickly grasping at the excuse to leave the ballroom.

As I followed my brother out the front door, I saw Theodore standing in front of another young lady, bowing slightly before accepting her dance card.

The cad obviously knew good manner. He just chose not to use them with me.

39

CAMERON

I sat at the desk, my screenplay open on my computer. My top hat sat on one side of my computer and my sister's letters on the other.

I told myself I was using them for inspiration, but in truth I knew that I was trying to solve a puzzle. The puzzle of time travel.

It was a mystery how and why it worked… and when.

And with whom.

I picked up one of my sister's letters. They were written on a special kind of paper—alkaline—with a special kind of ink that was supposed to last centuries. Not sure how they knew that, but I wasn't the scientist.

Since the letters were in good shape and readable, it seemed to have worked.

I picked up the first one and read it again for the hundredth time.

Dear Jonathan,

. . .

If you are reading this letter, then you know that I have gone back in time. It worked.

I so hope you found this letter. It makes me happy that you know I've made it to the past safely.

I didn't get to say goodbye and I'm sorry for that. But we talked about this and I know you understand. Still I miss you terribly and wish that you were here with me.

Please tell the rest of the family that I love them.

Take care of yourself and know that I love you.

Sophia

Sitting back in my chair, I analyzed the words.

It worked.

Grandpa was right. She had known how to go back in time.

And she and Grandpa had set it up for her to leave this letter for him behind the window frame.

He'd found it as soon as she had gone missing.

How had he known?

I tapped absently on my computer keyboard, letting my thoughts wander.

Then Grandpa returned to the window frame, twice more to find more letters from Sophia written over the years. I didn't let myself think about what it meant that she now lived—had lived—in the past.

The window frame was like a kind of mailbox.

A person could go there at any time and possibly find a letter from Sophia.

My fingers froze.

Go there at any time.

Then I remembered the woman's words. The woman from *The Haberdashery.*

Try the window.

I pushed back in my chair, dashed from the room, and took the stairs two at the time.

Breathing heavily, I knocked on Grandpa's door.

Sophia would know about me by now. About me and Isabella.

She would know.

And she had the answer.

40

ISABELLA

I sat in the carriage across from Sophia and Nathan. Sophia's face was slightly flushed.

"Are you alright?" I asked.

"Yes," she said, with a quick glance at Nathan. "I'm wonderful."

I sensed that there was something she wasn't saying. Nathan just shrugged when I looked at him questioningly. Apparently he did not know what it was either.

"Isabella," she said. "I think I may have figured out a way for this to work."

"For what to work?" My heart raced with possibilities.

She put a hand on my shoulder.

"But first I need to know something," she said, looking into my eyes.

"Okay," I nodded.

"I understand that you don't know my brother very well."

"True." I nodded, biting my bottom lip. But sometimes love only took an instant.

"I need to know how you feel about him. Truly feel about him."

I closed my eyes. Sophia was asking me for a reason. I sensed it was a very important reason.

My eyes were moist when I opened them and met her gaze again.

"He's all I can think about. I only came tonight because my father insisted."

"You love him?"

I nodded.

"You're in love with him?"

I nodded again.

I thought about him constantly. Replayed the moments we'd had together. Imagined what it would feel like to be reunited with me. Daydreamed about a future with him.

"Even though I know we may never be together, I can't fight it." I blushed at my own words, but I kept going. I sensed that this was very important. Otherwise, she and Nathan would not have sought me out tonight. They would have waited.

Sophia nodded.

"I can't stop thinking about him. He's the only man I've ever wanted to be with. The only man I'll ever want to be with."

"I think I know how to help you," she said, with excitement in her voice.

I blinked back unshed tears.

"There is a key," she said. "But it's in the future. The key can be used to go through time. I didn't have to use it, but I know a way to use it."

"How do you know this?" Nathan asked.

"Vaughn," Sophia told her husband.

"Vaughn? What? How?"

"I'll tell you later."

"Isabella," she said. "Do you want me to help you?"

"Yes," I said. "of course. When?"

"There's no time like the present."

41

CAMERON

I hadn't been in the guest room since I'd been here. It hurt me too much to be in the room Sophia had called her own. But now I had good reason to be here.

I brought a straight back chair over for Grandpa to sit on and I knelt on the floor.

He handed me his little pry bar.

"This is it?" I asked, indicating that section of the window frame that had been recently repaired. I already knew it was. Not only had Grandpa pointed it out to me, but the wood was a different color.

I was nervous. Both nervous and excited.

And the damn thing felt bittersweet.

I might find a way back in time to be with the woman I could not stop thinking about. Isabella.

At the same time, I'd be reunited with my sister. But if this worked, I would never see Grandpa again.

"Go ahead," Grandpa said.

I wiped my palm on my jeans and nodded.

Then I carefully slipped the little prybar beneath the wood.

The new wood lifted easily without breaking. Grandpa had not nailed it very tightly.

I suspected he'd known that he would be back.

If I were him, I'd probably check the damn thing at least once a day.

But Grandpa had an enormous amount of patience. Something I had not developed yet. Or maybe it was just because this could be a life changing event for me.

A little folded piece of paper fell out.

I picked it up off the floor with trembling hands and handed it out to Grandpa.

"Nope," he said. "This one's yours."

"How do you know?"

"Too many signs for it not to be."

"Okay," I said, carefully unfolded the paper. It was more of that alkaline paper and special ink.

Dear Grandpa and Cameron,

It took me awhile to figure out how to get this information to you. Now it just seems crazily simple.

"Sounds like Sophia," I said, with a little smile.

"It's her," Grandpa said, looking over my shoulder.

I kept reading.

I don't know if this will work to go back in time, but it worked to get me from the past to the future. I was going to try it, but I didn't have to.

By the way, Grandma Vaughn is the one who told me this. Here's what she told me:

Put the key in the clock. Then in the second between the lightning flash and following thunder, turn the clock back one hour.

I really, really hope this works. If it does, we'll see you soon.

Isabella and I are waiting.

Love you both,

Sophia

I HANDED THE LETTER TO GRANDPA. WAITED WHILE HE READ THE letter.

"That's it?" I asked.

He nodded.

"It sounds so simple."

"Nothing simple about it," he said.

"What do you mean?"

He took off his glasses and looked at me.

"Now you have to wait for a thunderstorm."

42

ISABELLA

Three months later

I walked alone on the dirt road toward the house. Large oak trees, laced with silvery strings of moss, canopied the road.

It was early morning, before anyone else was up. Something I did every morning now.

I liked the alone time. Liked having time to think my own thoughts without anyone else's opinions intruding on mine.

It had been three months since Sophia had written the letter and put it inside the window frame. A genius idea.

It was hard to imagine someone finding her letter nearly two hundred years in the future, but she was convinced they would.

She already had one letter in there, so she just added this one next to it and nailed the frame back down.

So now I waited.

Cameron had to get the letter first.

Then he had to wait for a thunderstorm.

There were so many unknowns. So many variables.

He had to still be there at the house to get the letter. Sophia had explained that her brother didn't live in the house with their Grandpa.

And… this was one I kept to myself. He had to want to come back in time. He had to care enough about me enough to give up his career… his work… everything… to come back in time.

It almost felt like too much to ask of anyone. What would he do here?

Sophia said he was a writer. But not books. Something sort of like plays, she'd said.

She hadn't told me much. Said he could explain it better. When he got here.

She was convinced that he would come back in time.

But I wasn't so easily convinced.

Whatever would be would be.

If he did not come back, then I would become an old maid.

I did not mind. Not really. I would definitely prefer to have Cameron come back, but if he didn't, I would content myself with my books, needlepoint, and piano.

I would not marry anyone else.

I couldn't do that.

Not when there would always be a chance that he could come back in time.

According to Sophia, for her, at least, time travel had not been linear.

It could be twenty years before he got her letter and found his way here.

Or he might not come now, but decide to come later in life.

He might decide to wait. Even if he came back when we were in our old age, I would be here for him.

He had not asked me to wait.

Some would say I was wasting my life.

But I refused to compromise. There was only one man for me.

One good thing had come out of this. My parents had stopped pressuring me to find someone to marry.

I picked up my pace.

There were dark clouds coming in from the southwest.

I wanted to get back home before the bottom fell out of the clouds.

43

CAMERON

Waiting for a thunderstorm took some pressure off me.

Knowing what I was waiting for gave me something concrete to grasp in a universe that had no logic.

So I locked myself into a routine. Go for a run. Breakfast with Grandpa. Shower.

Then I buried myself in my work. I didn't even care that I was technically out work. At least as much out of work as a writer could be.

I had enough money saved up that I didn't have to worry about it for a long time to come.

I'd had my belongings packed up, my furniture sold, and my condo in California put up for sale.

Now my belongings were on a truck on their way over here. I really didn't know what I was going to do with it all.

Probably just go through it and toss it.

But there might be a few things in there that I wanted to keep.

Or to give to someone else.

I'd tried to set up a time when my other two siblings could

come here so we could talk about the whole time-travel thing, but one or the other of them was too busy every weekend. I was okay with it, really.

The thought of trying to explain time travel to Mackenzie, a psychologist, especially made me nervous.

So I did not push.

Grandpa hired a young lady to come out three times a week to help his out. He reserved the option of having her come out more.

The plan was to get her trained, then after I went back in time, she could come out every day.

We'd told her that I was going to be traveling soon. For work. Something everyone understood and no one questioned.

I kept the Weather Channel on all the time. And I became something of an expert in the weather. I got to the point that I could actually feel dampness in the air before a rain.

But there had not been a single storm since the day we'd gotten the letter from Sophia explaining how to make the time travel happen.

I was ready. I was ready, but time was not.

So I lost myself in my work.

In the evenings, after Grandpa and I finished television, I spent an hour or so reading. Mostly on American history.

I did not want to go into this blind.

Maybe it wasn't fair for me to go back with knowledge of what was going to happen.

I mostly wanted to know what was going on in the 1830s so I didn't come across as a complete idiot. I wanted to be up on current events. As current as a man could be on something hundreds of years in the past.

It seemed like a lot of history got rewritten over time, so it was hard for me to know what was accurate and what wasn't.

I kept the photograph of Isabella on my desk… and made it the screensaver on my phone. I memorized every feature.

She inspired my writing, though I had to admit that I never expected anything to come of what I was writing.

When I did go to the past, I wouldn't be taking my manuscript with me.

So I wrote specific instructions for what to do with it when I was gone and tucked it under my computer.

Then I tucked all that depressing stuff away and focused on my future that just so happened to be in the past.

Today as I was coming back from my morning run, my phone chimed with a weather alert. I had five weather apps on my phone, so I didn't miss any updates.

They didn't always agree with each other.

But all five of them were going off.

I dashed upstairs and jumped into the shower. It threw off my routine, but I couldn't risk not being ready.

Gathering up my top hat, cravat, and walking cane, I took them downstairs to leave next to the clock.

I checked to be sure the key was still there, then went into the kitchen.

Grandpa sat there reading the newspaper, looking as though nothing was the least bit different.

I forced myself to be calm. It wasn't the first false alarm I'd had.

I was just ready for it to be the last.

"Did you see the weather?" he asked.

"Got five different alerts," I said, pouring myself a cup of coffee.

"The Weather Channel is blowing up with alerts, too."

I see that, stopping to look at the radar.

"This might be it," I said.

44

ISABELLA

The house was crowded with people wearing decorative masks over their eyes.

It was the Becquerel's annual Harvest Moon Ball. They'd added masks this year to give their party a bit of New Orleans flavor. It was kind of them, but unnecessary really, for them to work so hard at making us feel at home.

I was the one who seemed to like it the least, but I no longer cared. In fact, I was grateful that we had moved. If we had not moved here, I would not have met Cameron.

I stood at the punch bowl—a strawberry watermelon flavor tonight—and watched as the dancers waltzed around the room.

I wore a lovely lavender gown tonight with a silver overlay, all belling around me in a full hoop skirt. My mask matched the dress in silver with lavender trim.

"You should dance," Sophia said, joining me at the punch table.

"Sophia?" I recognized her voice. "What are you doing here?"

"Nathan and I decided to walk over." She shrugged. "It was an excuse to dress up."

"I guess it can be nice to dress up once in a while."

She took a cup and sipped.

"This is good," she said. "The weather seems warm tonight."

"It is unseasonable warm," I said, grateful that she didn't bring up dancing again.

If Cameron were here, I would gladly dance the night away. But not with anyone else.

A waiter came by. Offered us glasses of champagne.

I took one of the glasses from him, but Sophia waved the server away.

"This is good," I said. "Would you like to try it?"

"No," she said, leaning forward. "I can't have any."

"Why not?"

"I'm with child."

I gasped, then squeezed her in a hug.

"I'm so wonderfully happy for you and Nathan."

"Me too," she said. "You're going to be an aunt."

I grinned. My first niece or nephew.

"I would dance," she said. "But Nathan is still teaching me. You're lucky."

"How?" I asked warily. "You learned as a child."

"That is true." I lowered my voice. "Do people not dance in the future?"

"Rarely like this," she said.

"How do they dance then?"

Sophia scrunched her nose. "Actually it looks a lot like hopping."

"Hopping?"

"Sorry," Sophia said. "Nathan is waving me over."

I wanted to know more about this hopping dance, but she took off through the crowd toward Nathan.

I set the champagne down, then moving away from the punch table to get out of the way, found an empty seat on a little sofa in front of the window.

Men and women, many of them I knew by name, but just as many, maybe more, I did not know, floated by as they glided past in a graceful waltz.

I sighed as I imagined dancing with Cameron.

Would he know how to dance properly or would he only know how to…hop?"

I smiled to myself as I imagined standing out on the dance floor with Cameron. Hopping.

I giggled behind my gloved hand, thankful no one was watching me.

Amused by my own thoughts, I sipped my punch.

The waltz ended and the dancers scattered, mostly toward the punch table. The music stopped as the orchestra players took a break as well.

A man sat on the sofa next to me. I only saw him out of the corner of my eyes.

Theodore, I thought, bristling.

Could the man not take no for an answer?

"Do you have any room on that dance card?" he asked.

"Why is it you think you can be so informal with me?" Especially when he obviously knew proper manners.

I turned and looked at him. His mask was solid black with silver trim. It actually looked like one of the ones Momma had made. I'd helped her make some of them.

He grinned and my heart did funny little flips.

"My apologies," he said.

I peered at him, my throat suddenly dry. It was hard to recognize people wearing these masks, but this was not Theodore.

He sounded nothing like Theodore.

Mon Dieu.

"Cameron?" I whispered on a barely audible breath.

He stood up, tucking his walking cane beneath his left arm and held out his right hand.

When I lightly touched my gloved fingers to his hand, he took hold of my hand to assist me to my feet.

He pulled me close and I looked into his unbelievably deep blue eyes. Eyes that I had fallen in love with.

Leaning close, he whispered in my ear. "Can I have this dance?" he asked.

"There's no music," I said.

He leaned back, looking at me questioningly.

"Really?" He asked. "Are you sure? Because I hear the most beautiful music right now."

I smiled.

"Yes," I said. "I hear it, too."

45

CAMERON

Isabella and I stood together on the back veranda. The evening breeze tugging her hair loose from her up-do.

"Where did you get that mask?" she asked, running a finger along the outside edge of my mask.

"Your mother handed it to me. Said I couldn't go the ball without one."

"I thought it looked familiar," she said. "I think I helped make this one."

"I see," I said. I was still trying to grasp the realization that turning the key had actually worked.

As the storm came closer and closer, I put on my top hat and cravat, grabbed my cane, and went to stand in front of the clock.

I'd used the method outlined in Sophia's letter… right in the middle of a thunderstorm… and it had worked.

I'd watched Grandpa vanish right in front of my eyes. But it hadn't been him who had vanished. It had been me.

"You need to find Sophia. Let her know you're here," she said.

"I will," I said.

"She's here tonight," she said.

I pulled her close.

"I'll find her in a little bit." I took off my hat.

"Where did you get that hat?" Isabella asked, covering her mouth with one hand.

"Hey," I said. "What's wrong with my hat?"

"Nothing," she said. "But it's a little bit out of style."

I turned the hat over and looked at it.

"It looks like everyone else's."

"Look," she said. "the brim on yours is wider."

"I didn't even notice."

"That went out of style two years ago."

"Oh," I said. "Two years."

It was such a minute difference. Something only someone who lives in this time would be aware of. Isabella would notice.

Two years ago was a long time for her.

For me, it was early 1800s or late 1800s. Not enough differences to point out. Everyone wore a top hat until they didn't. Next chapter in the history book.

I looked into her beautiful emerald green eyes framed by thick dark lashes. Her plush pink lips curved into an impish little smile.

"Can you stay?" she asked.

I swept my thumb lightly across her lips and her eyes drifted closed in response.

"There's something I have to do first."

"Okay," she said. "I understand."

She opened her eyes and looked at me so sweetly it practically tore my heart into a million pieces.

To think that time almost kept us apart.

I pressed my lips against hers and the earth seemed to shift beneath my feet.

"Yes," I said against her lips. "I can stay."

46

ISABELLA

After a tearful reunion between Sophia and Cameron, a reunion that brought tears to my eyes, Cameron and I walked in the garden behind the main house.

The strong clean scent of daffodils scented the air and lively music spilled from the house.

For the first time in forever, the happy music warmed my heart, making me feel almost giddy.

And I was not a giddy person.

But walking along the garden path, holding hands with Cameron, my perspective was forever altered.

"I need to tell you something," he said as we walked along the shadowed path a cool evening breeze wafting over us.

"What?" I asked, looking over at him. He was so handsome. I could barely believe my good fortune in finding him.

I truly believed that my resistance in allowing any man to court me was the universe's way of keeping me for him.

"I don't have any money," he said. "And I don't have a job."

"Oh," I said. "Is that all?"

"Your father won't be very happy about it, I'm sure."

The music changed to something more serious and I actually missed the happy music.

"Actually, my father knows that you're from the future," I said. "So I don't think he expects you to come with much."

"I hope that's true," he said. "What about you? Does that matter to you? I can probably write some stories and sell them."

"Your sister said you write plays."

"Something like that," he said with a grin. "Maybe I'll try my hand at a novel."

"You can write a novel?" I asked, in awe.

"I might have to get you to help me learn to use a quill," I said with a little laugh.

"I have excellent penmanship," I said. "I can help you."

"That sounds wonderful," He grinned and kissed my fingertips.

"My family will take care of us," I said. "I'm sure of it. Don't worry."

He stopped and, taking both my hands, stood directly in front of me.

"I won't worry if you won't worry," he said.

"Deal." I smiled.

He put a hand behind my neck and pressed his lips against my forehead.

So soft. So sweet.

We walked and talked as the music was nothing but a lingering memory and the moon was lost behind wispy morning clouds.

We made plans and we shared dreams.

"I don't ever want to say goodnight," he said as we reached the quiet back veranda and stood at the bottom of the stairs.

"Where will you sleep?" I asked, not wanting to say goodnight either.

"I'll sleep in the library," he said.

"I don't want you to leave." I grasped his hands.

He wrapped me in his arms and tucked my head beneath his chin.

"It's only temporary, my love. I'll speak with your father in the morning."

I nodded against his chest.

"If one of us accidentally falls through the rip in time," I said. "at least we know how to get back."

"I'm not going anywhere," he said. "I'm exactly where I want to be."

He pressed his hands against my face.

"Don't worry," he said. "And I'll make you a promise."

"Okay."

He kissed me, then shifted back just enough to look into my eyes.

"I promise to love you until the end of time."

The rest of the world faded away as he kissed me again.

Cameron was my love and I was his. Not even time itself could keep us apart.

Keep Reading for a Preview of Destined in the Twilight…

DESTINED IN THE TWILIGHT PREVIEW

Chapter 1
Mackenzie Becquerel

I sat on the sofa in my Grandpa Jonathan's parlor, his cat looking up at me with obvious curiosity.

The cat was solid white with bright blue eyes. A hairball with eyes.

When did Grandpa get a cat, anyway?

I didn't need this additional piece of evidence that I had not been to visit my Grandpa enough.

When my phone vibrated in my jacket pocket, I glanced at the round analog clock on the wall across the room.

I didn't have any appointments right now, but it could be a client. Or a student.

Grandpa had stepped out to the foyer to answer his phone and I could hear him talking to someone, but couldn't understand his words.

The cat meowed at me.

I gave in to what I knew was a common and irritating addiction and checked the message on my phone.

It was not a client. It was my sister, Victoria.

VICTORIA: *Did you make it there yet?*

ME: *Yes. Waiting for Grandpa to get off the phone.*

I tucked the phone back in my pocket. I'd promised Victoria that I'd let her know when I got here.

Unfortunately for her, I was not good at that sort of thing.

But Victoria had generalized anxiety disorder. She'd always had anxiety, but since my sister Sophia disappeared ten years ago, it had gotten worse.

And now, we had not heard from our brother in over a month.

That's why I was here.

I knew Cameron had been here. He'd sent me a text telling me that he was spending some time here with Grandpa and working on a project.

Unlike Victoria, I hadn't worried when I hadn't heard from him in a couple of weeks. Cameron was like me in that way. He didn't like to check in with others when he could take care of himself.

But after a few days of no response from Cameron by text with calls going straight to voicemail, I had eventually called Grandpa.

He'd talked in vague phrases, suggesting that Victoria and I come for a visit.

But I'd asked specifically about Cameron.

Grandpa said Cameron's car was here, but he wasn't.

Since Grandpa was getting up in age and had been through a lot of stress lately—with his wife dying a few years ago, then my sister vanishing from his home—I knew I had to check on him.

If he was getting dementia, he'd have to be moved into a facility.

Since all us—me, Cameron, and Victoria—had careers, we could not take care of him.

My private practice was going gangbusters.

I'd had to reschedule a day of clients just to come here for two days. I was going to be working extra hours for at least a week, maybe two, to catch up. Some people worked five days a week with weekends off. Not me. I worked six days a week. Taught a class in the evenings and used Sundays to catch up on progress notes and prepare lectures for the following week.

In between clients I answered student texts. While I graded online exams, I took texts and calls from clients.

To say I had a busy schedule was an understatement.

Victoria suggested I work on boundaries. But Victoria had never taught today's instant gratification students, nor had she worked with clients in a crisis.

I did not fault her for not understanding. Most people couldn't.

I blamed it all on the Internet. Most websites had some kind of instant chat capabilities. We, as a society, were trained to get immediate responses on most things.

So when a student sent a message of any sort, they expected a response right away.

Not their fault either and I didn't judge them for it.

I was the same way.

But no one in my family understood.

Hence the boundaries criticisms that came phrased all sorts of different ways.

I did what it took to be successful.

Even if that meant I spent twelve hours a day tethered to my electronic devices, turning them off for fifty minute intervals between clients.

The cat meowed at me again.

"What?" I asked. "Am I in your chair?"

I stood up and the cat immediately jumped into my chair

where I had been sitting.

"I guess that's a yes."

This was going to be an interesting visit.

Chapter 2
Andrew Laurent

May 1854

I RACED ACROSS THE FALLOW FIELDS, THE MOVEMENT OF THE horse powerful beneath me.

I liked that and the feel of the wind in my face.

And admittedly, I liked speed.

My horse, Lightning Bug, had been with me for years. I was pretty sure he was used to my occasional needs to race across a field.

My sister, Isabella, had named him. I'd been planning to change it to something more masculine, but I just never got around to it. So Lightning Bug had stuck.

There were worse names as far as names went.

I pulled on the reins, letting the horse know that we could stop now.

We walked slowly down the dirt road leading up to the front of my uncle's house, known as the Becquerel Estate.

I'd grown up in New Orleans, but my family had packed up and moved here last year after a mishap with our property down there. The estate house had burned and the city house had to be sold to pay off remaining debt. There was enough money left for a new start.

My father was in the process of to building his own house on some of mother's property adjacent to my uncle's.

In the meantime, we all lived in the big three-story house

with my cousins.

Even though the house was plenty big for all us—two big families—I preferred spending time at the garçonnière, my cousin's bachelor's apartment. But lately he had begun wanting more privacy, so I was currently living here in one of the many guest rooms in the big old house.

As I rode beneath the large oak trees draping over the road, I thought maybe I'd go into town tonight.

Have a whiskey. Maybe go over to Natchez Under the Hill. It was a rather dangerous place, all in all, but I liked it. I actually liked the little thrill of danger that went with going someplace my father would have my head for going.

It wasn't that I was rebellious. It was just that I was used to live in New Orleans. Living here in the northern part of Mississippi after growing up in New Orleans, was a big adjustment and I didn't know if would ever be ready to live the boring life of a cotton planter.

Instead, I worked hard during the day and played hard in the evenings.

Reaching the front of the house, I slid off the horse, looped the reins over the hitching post, and ran up the steps.

My cousin, Emma, met me at the door.

"There you are," she said. "I've been looking for you."

Emma was rather annoying as far as cousins went. And adding her to her general annoyingness, her favorite pastime was playing the piano.

She played it all the time, especially delighting in playing for guests in the evenings.

She was a good enough player. But sometimes sitting there listening to her playing the piano for hour after hour was worse than watching paint dry.

"Mother is having some guests over tonight and she wants you to be here," Emma said with obvious excitement.

My spirits crumbled. If my Aunt Eloise wanted me here for

dinner, then I would be here for dinner. Aunt Eloise was hands down the most frightening woman I knew.

I kicked the dirt off my boots with my walking stick and followed Emma inside.

"What time?" I asked, trying to gauge if I would have time to go into town after the guests left.

"They'll be here at six," she said. "And after that, they want me to play the piano for them."

"Of course they do." I tempered my response with a smile.

So there would be more paint drying tonight and I wouldn't be going into town after all.

Chapter 3
Mackenzie

GRANDPA, APPARENTLY, HAD HIRED AN ASSISTANT NAMED TRACIE.

As Tracie brought in a tray with hot tea along with some crackers and cheese, it occurred to me that I could use an assistant myself.

Sometimes I even forgot to eat. An assistant could help with that kind of thing.

"Have a seat, Tracie," I said, sitting in an armchair. "Tell me about yourself."

Tracie's eyes widened.

"Yes ma'am," she said, sitting on the edge of a chair across from me.

Classic type A personality, I decided.

"How long have you been working for Grandpa?"

"Not long," she said. "only a couple of weeks."

"And you live here?"

"Oh no ma'am," she said. "But if you need me to, I can make

arrangements to be here more."

"Not necessary," I said with a smile. "What you and Grandpa have worked out is fine, I'm sure."

"I should go check on him," she said.

"Okay," I said. "Nice to meet you."

"Thank you," Tracie said, jumping up and leaving the room. "You too."

Tracie obviously had a lot of insecurities, but her eagerness to please no doubt made up for it.

Standing up, I walked to the window. The cat got up and walked with me.

"What's your name, Kit Kat?" I asked.

The cat didn't answer.

"I guess I'll call you Kit Kat then until I find out otherwise. Seems you're the only one who wants to talk to me at the moment."

Kit Kat just blinked and rubbed against my legs.

Looked like he wasn't really talking right now either.

The wind blew through the trees outside, sending leaves and moss scattering across the lawn.

Looked like Grandpa had let the yard maintenance go. Another sign that he was developing dementia.

A few minutes later Grandpa joined me in the parlor.

"I'm sorry, Mackenzie," he said. "I had to take that."

"It's no problem," I said, with a smile. "I'm in no hurry."

Not until tomorrow anyway. Then I would be ready to go. To get home so I could catch up on some work. Get ready for next week.

I walked over and sat back down on the sofa. Kit Kat followed, jumping up to sit next to me.

"When did you get a cat?" I asked.

"Last week," he said, sitting across from me. "Tracie and I went down to the pound and rescued him.

I quickly squashed down the little spurt of jealousy mixed

with guilt that someone outside of family had to take Grandpa to the pound to rescue a pet.

When Grandpa patted his knee, Kit Kat ran over and jumped in his lap.

"I think he likes you," I said.

"He's my buddy," Grandpa said, rubbing the cat's ears.

"Good. I'm glad you have him."

"And I'm glad you could come. Is Victoria okay?"

"Yes. She's busy with work, as always."

"That's how it is with doctors."

Grandpa got points for remembering that Victoria was a doctor.

"So… as I said, I haven't heard from Cameron lately. I'm getting a little concerned about him."

"I'm sure he's good," Grandpa said. "I don't think he's going back California."

"Oh." Cameron loved California, especially his job. "What about his condo?"

"He sold it."

Sold it. That was a big move. "So he moved. Do you know where he went? Is he living here with you?"

"His car is here," Grandpa said, giving me that vague answer about the car again.

"Okay," I said with utmost patience. "If his car is here, but he isn't, how is he getting around? Did he get another car?"

"Do you want some tea?" Grandpa asked, not answering my question.

"Sure." Though truthfully I would have preferred a latte right about now. Something to stall out the headache I felt coming on.

"How often does Tracie get to come out?" I asked.

"Three times a week," he said.

"That's not very often," I said. "If you need her to come out more often, I can help with the money."

"I'm not hurting for money," Grandpa waved a hand, dismissing my offer. "Got more than I can spend. Ever."

"I see. So do you have plans to at least spend some of it?"

"I'll spend it on caregivers and on food and such. Doesn't take much to live."

I jumped onto clinician alertness. If Grandpa was suicidal, then I definitely needed to intervene.

"She and I are going shopping nest week for groceries. I don't drive anymore."

I knew that. We all knew that.

"Someone told me that," I said. "it's commendable that you willingly gave up your car keys." I really didn't know if he gave them up willingly or not, but I wanted him to think I knew that it had been willingly.

"I don't know about that," he said. "But it was time."

"Well, if you thought it was time, then I have to agree."

"Getting older is not for the faint of heart," Grandpa said, tapping his knee with the back of his hand.

"No, wouldn't think so. I just hope you feel good enough to move around and do what you want to do."

"I do alright," he said. "Having Tracie here to help out helps. Especially without Sophia or Cameron around."

"Just make sure you do your exercises," I said.

Grandpa nodded and I got a sense he was merely appeasing me.

I would have to spend more time with him to really know if he had dementia. Except for the way he talked about Cameron, he seemed to be holding his own.

I needed to back up and run at it again.

"When was the last time you saw Cameron?" I asked.

"Come on," Grandpa said. "Let's make something to eat."

Keep Reading Destined in the Twilight…

Kathryn Kaleigh is the author of sixty-eight novels, over one hundred short stories, and many collections.

kathrynkaleigh.com

www.ingramcontent.com/pod-product-compliance
Lightning Source LLC
Chambersburg PA
CBHW030337310726
48979CB00001B/72
9781647913939